This book is dedicated to the strong women that]
the way I live my life; may god bless you all.

Nanny Winnie the highest accolade I could give you was taking your name as an author; I miss you so much.

And to my father, there is not a day that we don't smile when we talk about you, your life lives on through your grandchildren, you will never be forgotten until we meet again.

Chapter one

"Ronnie get your ass out of the bed and make me a cup of tea!" Ronnie opened one eye sleepily and stretched slowly before putting her feet out from under her old blankets onto the cold wooden floor her feet were like little blocks of ice, at 11 years old she was more clued up than half the women that lived in her block and it showed in her eyes, her bedroom was sparse no dolls, teddys or love was put into it, it was as neglected as the slightly built child that slept in it. The floral wallpaper that the previous tenants had put up was slowly peeling in the corners discoloured and lifeless from the sun that was streaming through the curtain less window it made Ronnie squint as her eyes got accustomed to the brightness.

She quickly ran down the stairs and put the kettle on and looked in the fridge to see if there was any milk or food as her belly rumbled angrily, she went to bed hungry and woke up starving. Wrinkling her nose at the smell that hit her square in the face she shook her head in dismay as per usual it was grim and slim pickings, a bit of cheese and a jar of old mustard, pulling the tiny bit of milk out her nose curled when she sniffed the bottle "sod that it's curdled right up" she muttered she tipped it down the sink trying not to heave, shopping was definitely not Nancy's forte, "black tea it is then" Ronnie turned the kettle on and looked in the cupboard for a cup, she heard the bed springs on her mother's bed creak above her as Nancy pulled herself up and out of the bed, Ronnie waited with baited breath, that was the thing with her mother you never knew what frame of mind she was in, as dolly the next door neighbour stated the other night "that fucker can have a fight with her own fingernails ark at her" as she watched Nancy staggering back from the pub with Billy her latest paramour on her arm, drunk as a proverbial skunk, singing at the top of her lungs, waking up half the street.

Nancy walked downstairs into the kitchen slowly like she was wounded, her head was pounding vodka was not her friend! as she sat down heavily at the kitchen table Ronnie looked up at her mother's face, she still wore last night's make up, it was smudged and hanging off her like a washed out clown Ronnie felt a pang of sadness at what was staring back at her. Nancy knew her eyes and chest were her main assets, large and electric and standing to attention as many of her punters stated but she could see the cheeks that were now starting to go slightly puffy from the drink and the lines around her eyes and mouth were deepening, the drink and drugs were taking a toll on her pretty face and her body her figure which was her main asset was not as firm as it used to be, luckily Nancy had something that not many women had, that inner sexiness that men loved they were drawn to her like a moth to the flame, she knew how to pull them and use them but she never cared for any of them they were easy marks as far as she was concerned. Sensing that her daughter was scrutinizing her she barked in her deep gravelly voice "where the fuck is my tea my mouth feels like its spitting feathers" Ronnie quickly placed the cup in front of her mum, "there's no milk it was off so it will have to be black" "better than a kick up the ass I suppose" Nancy replied, "pass me my bag babe I need a fag" Ronnie dutifully went and picked her bag up from the floor where Nancy had dropped it and took it in to the kitchen, Nancy pulled out her Benson and Hedges and lit one up taking a long pull on the cigarette and slowly blew the smoke out that filled her lungs, she looked over at Ronnie thoughtfully "don't bother going to school today I need you to tidy this tip up Billy is coming round later and I want this place to sparkle"

Nancy didn't care that Ronnie had no breakfast and now the one meal that she could count on, that happened to be at school was going up in smoke. Nancy was selfish and slapdash, and when it came to motherhood, Ronnie's needs were so low in the pecking order they didn't exist. Nancy cared about herself and that was it. Billy was Nancy's latest love interest a local pimp and class A dealer, her eyes sparkled thinking about him as far as she was concerned the sun shone out of his ass, he made sure he slid her a few wraps of coke to make the nights a bit easier, knowing it kept her sweet and bought her loyalty, and for this she looked past his reputation. Billy was known to be a spiteful bastard to his girls especially when they didn't play the game and fall in line, at the moment she looked at him through rose tinted glasses believing she was the girl that had finally snared his heart. Nancy smirked to herself she didn't get it twisted, she didn't love him, she had an inner cunning, a devious nature and made sure she was rinsing all she could from him without making it too obvious, she wanted to cultivate him and get what she could, it was a dance they both played and she would play it for all it was worth, she knew deep down he wasn't stupid and probably see her as another work horse to add to his stable, he would soon bore with her and move onto his next trick that he was pulling into the life, but she was in for the ride.

Nancy was very realistic she knew she still had a few more years on her back and Billy was happy to put her in one of his massage parlours as long as she kept the punters happy and paid her rent he didn't give a fuck, all Nancy wanted was the security of having a protector as it was getting harder on the streets her nerves were beginning to fray. It was only last week one of the young girls was found brutally beaten and left for dead down Toynbee street and it scared her, they had worked the same pavement, she knew the punters wanted the younger girls that would give a blow job for a tenner, the addicts did anything they could to stick a quick needle in their arm, finding out that Betty was dead was the push she finally needed. Nancy was fed up with standing in the dark waiting for a quick fumble up a wall so being with Billy was a match made in heaven they both had a use for each other, both were as happy playing the game, Billy had a few irons in the fire and if this latest little deal worked it would set him up and she being his current amour would give her the added kudos around the neighbourhood that she craved.

Looking over at Ronnie, Nancy felt a quick flicker of shame, Ronnie was a skinny little thing with big blue eyes and a dusting of freckles across her upturned nose,

3

Nancy didn't know who Ronnie's dad was and didn't care, she definitely got her eyes from her mother just as she had but that was where the similarity's ended, Nancy was a runaway and was already working the streets when she fell with Ronnie, she worked that pavement until she was too big to carry on brazenly telling anyone to fuck off that voiced their opinion or disgust, she didn't look at Ronnie as a blessing she looked at her as a hinderance, a pain in the ass that was holding her back, but deep inside she felt that small nugget of love that stopped her from giving her up. Nancy had foisted Ronnie onto anyone that would watch her as soon as she was able to get back on the streets and in the clubs, disappearing for days at a time, the bond between mother and child was virtually non-existent, Nancy didn't know how to bond she was never shown it herself. Social services were always on her case but the neglect was never bad enough for them to take little Ronnie, she had never laid a hand on her she was just slapdash with care, she told herself the money she claimed in family allowance come in handy as did the next to nothing rent was part of the reason so she held onto little Ronnie but in her heart, she loved little Ronnie. The "life" had a tight grip on her, she didn't know any other way out, Nancy had become a night owl, a street walker, a hustler she lived for the darkness it was all she knew, it was a comforting blanket that she could wrap herself in.

"Ronnie stop fucking about and straighten this place up" Nancy looked around the worn out kitchen that didn't have a bit of space the ashtray was over flowing, make up from last night was strewn all over the sides, an empty bottle of vodka that was the left over from the night before was laying on its side where Nancy had knocked it over pissed up, no wonder my sides are hurting this morning, my liver has taken another beating, Nancy would never say it out loud but knew in her heart the drinking and coke was now like a runaway train in her life, reality was never her strongest point when it came to the drink. Looking at the sticky cup ring marks across the old glass kitchen table she stood up stretched and said to Ronnie "get cracking girl" as she walked back upstairs in desperate need of a cold shower, feeling like her head was about to cave in.

Ronnie as always was very resourceful she ended up melting the cheese on the crackers she found in the back of the cupboard and got to work steadily through the kitchen bleaching and shining as she went, humming away to herself, luckily the front room was not looking like a tornado had hit it, looking at the thick flock wall paper and big fireplace in the front room that was her mother's pride and joy Ronnie smiled, Nancy truly believed they were the height of good taste, the fireplace had been knocked up from some left over York stone that Tony the neighbour had nicked off a job. The sides were littered with ornaments from the market, cheap golden horses and clowns shone in the sun almost jostling for space, the sofas had seen better days and clashed with the wallpaper, but they were clean and comfortable. Opening the door and walking onto the small balcony Ronnie smelt the air of the east

4

end, their flat was in between Brick Lane and Columbia road, she had the best of both worlds, Brick lane for the bagels and pie mash from G Kelly's it was all a stone's throw away. Ronnie's world revolved around food she was always hungry and dreaming of her next meal, Columbia Road was just around the corner she walked there every Sunday just for the colours and smell of fresh cut flowers. Tomlinson Close was a typical council estate of the 80's it had the smell of bacon and wacky baccy permanently fermenting the air, there was clean washing constantly flapping on the lines in the yards and gardens below, the yards were the meeting place for the mothers. Leaning over the balcony Ronnie shouted hello to Sue the neighbourhood gossip who looked up and acknowledged Ronnie with a friendly wave, what Sue didn't know wasn't worth knowing, she knew everyone's business and sat outside her front door from morning till night with her tea, fags and her reggae playing in the background while regaling her stories to all the mothers that constantly graced her doorstep, if anything was hooky or freshly nicked from the back of the van or a local Tesco's, Sue was the women that was selling it thus making her very popular to everyone on the manor.

After her blast in the shower Nancy started to feel the blood pump back around her body and she started to feel a little less fragile, she had found a wrap of speed in her jeans and decided to bomb it back with the last dregs of vodka and coke that was left in her glass on her bedside. As she waited for the speed to kick in and give her the much needed energy she started to think about the day ahead and the meet that was going on in her home, she knew that Billy had business with the Donnelly's and that it was heavy duty but didn't care as long as she got a good drink from it, she had never met the Donnelly's but their reputation proceeded them, they could use her place as the meeting point to plan the skulduggery at hand. As the speed started to flow through her veins Nancy relaxed, turning her radio up full blast she started humming to Whitney Houston busily styling her hair and carefully applying her makeup trying to not overdo it and remind the men that she was a brass, her clothes were tossed everywhere as she pulled them from the wardrobe, she tried on different options before deciding on a tight fitting pair of jeans and her favourite silk blouse understated and classy was the look she was aiming for, spraying herself liberally with her knocked off Giorgio Armani she looked in the mirror, shaking her freshly blow dried hair and blew herself a kiss, "I look like fucking dynamite if I don't say so myself" and once again she was ready to face the world and get down to business chuckling to herself thinking yes I am the hostess with the mostest.

As Nancy walked down the stairs Ronnie had just finishing mopping the lino in the hallway she looked up and couldn't believe the transformation "mum you look gorgeous" she gaped at her mum with her mouth hanging open this wasn't the going to work look mum this was different, this was glamourous mum! Nancy feeling a bit more human smiled down at little Ronnie "thanks babes, listen I'm going to pop down to Sami's and get some bits in, how about some crusty bread bacon buttys, with a nice mug of tea?" Ronnie's face lit up with delight at the thought of fresh food "that would be handsome mum" she smiled. "do me a favour pop upstairs and sort my room out, give the bathroom a quick once over and I will be back in a jiffy ok" Ronnie nodded hurrying herself upstairs, the thought of a bacon sandwich gave her the much needed energy spirt.

Nancy walked to the lift humming to herself, thinking not long now and Billy will be round, I better get some good scotch and beers in as well, as the door opened the smell of ammonia made her take a step back, she shook her head she could never understand why people would take a piss on their own doorstep when they had a toilet literally ten feet from the lift door! scumbags she muttered the irony not lost on her that half her neighbours called her the same and ignored her for that same reason, she was classed as filth by most of the women in her road, not that it bothered her, unless they walked in her shoes who were they to judge? that was what she had always told herself, it was her protective layer that she cloaked herself in. As she stepped out of the block, she spotted Sue, "alright girl what's happening? have you got anything in?" Sue nodded as she reeled off her latest stock "I have some lovely beef, coffee, cheese, shampoos and make up if you're interested" Nancy nodded while she had a few quid she might as well stock up "do me up a parcel for a score and I will pick it up on the way back Hun" Sue nodded "no problem, did you hear about Mark in number 32? his been giving Anita you know the junkie prostitute one, I knew something was going on but his missus caught him with his pants down last night there's been absolute murders" Nancy laughed "it serves Theresa right she always was a stuck up fucker that thought she was better than all of us but to know her man's been giving a skag head one is karma as far as I'm concerned, and she better get her ass down the clinic as that Anita takes punters without protection, anyway just going to Sami's as Billy is coming round later so I'm just going to get some bits in" she see Sues eyes widen at the mention of Billy's name and walked off smug knowing that it would be all over the estate by the afternoon that she was seeing one of the faces of Bethnal Green, be it a unpopular one.

Nancy picked up a few bags of much needed supply's, she was a bit flush after rolling a punters wallet the night before, it was amazing how easy it was to slip a wallet off a man when he was going for gold between her legs. Nancy breezed into the house throwing all the bags on the table, "Ron come down and put this gear away and put the kettle on babe" sitting down heavily she lit another cigarette and blew the smoke out, speed always made her irritated "come on Ron get this bacon on I haven't got all day" her appetite had gone, the speed had well and truly kicked in but she knew she had to eat something even if it tasted of sawdust as she knew she was pulling an all nighter. Billy was guaranteed to have a pocket full of coke so once the business was over, she was off out to wherever the night took her, she rubbed her hands with glee, she was like a blood hound. She could smell the money that was in the air, ripe for the picking!

Ronnie finished making the sandwiches and poured the hot sweet tea into their old mismatched mugs and sat down to eat. She scoffed it down quickly blimey that hit the spot, she thought. She looked across at her mum and sensing something was not right "what's wrong mum you're well twitchy, you in trouble" Ronnie asked her mum sincerely. "No Ron but we have some people coming tonight so I want you to go down to Aunty Sues and stay there until they have gone, don't need you hanging about whilst Billy talks business putting a downer on everything, Sue won't mind" Ronnie nodded happily, she loved Aunt Sue's it was lovely and warm, she always had plenty of food and above all she had time for little Ronnie. "I will have a quick wash, mum square up the kitchen and get ready and go down to her after" Ronnie was eager to go downstairs and see her mates she knew she could play out the front till dark and Sue would watch over her.

After finishing her jobs and getting ready Ronnie run down the stairs no way was she using that shitty lift, it stunk to high heaven! She run out of the block and spotted her best friend Kelly who as always was waiting for her with the boys "you want to play run outs Ron?" Ronnie smiled back at her "of course I do but let me go to Aunt Sue's first" she ran along to Sue who was now drinking a little rum and coke and smiled "hello aunty, mum said can I stay with you tonight she has people over and she thinks it will be an all-nighter" Sue smiled at little Ronnie this dear little girl pulled at her heart strings as a mother of four boys she had a soft spot for her, she would kill for a girl like little Ronnie, a little diamond, thinking that Nancy was a lazy selfish fucker "sweetheart you know you can always stay at Aunty Sues, you are always welcome here your like one of my own" "Ronnie smiled back at her, eyes glistening with unshed tears unaccustomed to the show of affection she rushed at her all arms and legs to give her a cuddle, Sue hugged her back and genuinely wanted to cry she could feel her slight little body under her cheap clothes and squeezed her a little tighter, plastering a big smile on her face she held her and said " go on, you go and play with your mates and I will have a lovely bit of dinner waiting for you when you're done, take little Terry with you and keep an eye on him" Terry was Sue's youngest and last child he was beautiful with creamy brown skin and tight light curls, he was a beautiful mixed race boy that was protected and babied by his large family. As they all put it, he was the centre of their little universe.

Sue had caused a huge upset in her family when she had lost her heart to a gorgeous black man and had given birth to four boys in quick succession, just when she thought she was done, she had fallen with little Terry, she was proud of all her boys, their father Errol was a lovable rogue he disappeared for months on end but she didn't care she had her boys and that's all that mattered to her, she still had the odd snide remark and dirty look but she told anyone that was brave enough to confront her to go do one, she didn't give a flying fuck as she put it, but this little one he was her heartbeat, her pride and joy her last blessing "Terry, Ronnie's here for you come here babe and mummy will put your shoes on sweetheart, Ron don't go too far when you're playing no further than the green ok" Ronnie loved little Terry and nodded while smiling down at her handsome little prince "of course Aunty Sue I will take him and the football and we will play kick ups in the football pitch ok" bending down to little Terry Ronnie gave him a quick hug and put the football under one arm and held out her hand to take Terrys, as she walked towards the football pitch, Sue watched them walking off and smiled sadly, thinking for a girl that was given nothing by a selfish bitch like Nancy she would give anyone anything just to be loved, she would of loved a daughter like Ronnie.

Robert and Malcolm were sitting under the tree with some of the boys smoking a cheeky joint and drinking some beers, the air was heavy with menace, Roberts dad was a staunch National Front supporter and had just been laid off yet again, Robert was telling anybody that would listen that some black bastard had gone in and nicked his dads job, as he droned on to Malcolm and anyone that was in earshot of listening, "we have shaved our heads, wear the bomber jackets and boots for what? it's not a fucking fashion statement, we are showing our solidarity to the far right, Enoch Powell was right I'm telling you it won't be long and were going to be overrun with these fuckers" Malcolm was sitting there high on some lovely weed half listening as Robert ranted on thinking to himself, let's be honest your dad was given the sack because he was a drinker and was nicking the paint out of the depo, he was lucky he had got away with it for as long as he had, half the houses in Bethnal green had probably been painted with his hooky paint. Malcom yawned and stretched out hoping that Robert would run out of steam and just shut the fuck up, the weed was not even chilling Robert out he was getting more agitated as the day wore on "I'm telling you theses coons are gonna be the death of us if not them it's the paki's, were overrun with them, we have to rise up or we will be all be screwed, they already have the corner shops and now they're everywhere down the lane with their factory's and leather shops were being pushed out" Malcolm's looked on keeping his mouth shut, man this dude is really trying to kill my buzz he don't stop bitching, as he looked across the green his heart sunk he could see a little slip of a girl walking along holding onto a little boy with some other kids they were all laughing and joking, it wasn't this that worried him, looking at the boy you could see that he definitely had a lick of the tar brush as his mum would say, fuck! if Robert sees that kid his going to start the way his been all day this is going to be a nightmare trying to diffuse the situation before it started Malcolm jumped up straightened his braces and pulled on his green bomber jacket "come on lets go down the arches and see if Mickeys about I heard his got some pukka smoke" he looked down at Robert who hadn't seem to register what Malcolm was saying his eyes were transfixed on the kids that were walking towards them, "look at that he shouted pointing over at Ronnie and little Terry she's got a little half chat with her!" Ronnie registered the slur straight away, she pulled her shoulders back and let rip at the skin head, giving it to him with both barrels, she pulled terry protectively behind her and stood up straight and shouted, "what did you say you bald bastard, who the fuck do you think you are, look at you you're a hot mess mate you don't scare me! so do us all a favour and fuck off!" Malcolm was rendered speechless this slip of a girl was protecting the little chavvi and was standing there blatant in his face not even scared, he was in a quandary if he backed down he would look like a right mug, in his heart he knew he was taking the piss she was just a kid but Malcolm had always been spiteful by nature, before his head could engage he opened his mouth and shouted " I bet your mother is ashamed of you hanging around with that" Ronnie belly laughed at that, oh the irony! "so fucking what mate what you going to do about it, you're a fat ugly dickhead look at ya you have more rolls around your belly then Percy Ingles and your starting on a kid, you know what makes me laugh with dick heads like you if you was rushed into a hospital it would probably be a black nurse that had to wipe your fat ass, bet you wouldn't open your mouth to her would you! people like you make me sick" little Ronnie was now in full swing but she wouldn't back down for love nor money she was now starting to shake with anger. She didn't see Kelly slip off and run back up the field towards Sue's "Sue quick! quick! Ronnie's having a row with a skin head and his called little Terry horrible names, before Sue could even rise up her Tyrone and Roger flew out of the door and were running with bats in there hand, she always kept them handy by the door just in case she had any grief, Sue sat down and half smiled she knew her boys would take care of business, "go back and bring little Terry back with Ron the boys will soon sort them out" Kelly took off as fast as her feet could take her, no way was she missing out on this action wait until she told her mum and the kids in school tomorrow they won't believe it! Tomlinson close was never dull!

As Tyrone was running down the grass all her could hear was Ronnie's mouth, blimey who would of thought that little thing had a mouth like that she was turning the air blue! he was proud because she wasn't in the least bit scared and could definitely hold her own, he looked at Roger with his eyebrows raised a half smile on his face to them this was sport! and as if they had spoken out loud they nodded in a unspoken agreement, "Ronnie babe, take little Terry back to my mums and we will be right back" little Terry looked up at his big brothers and smiled, they were satisfied that he was looking unduly distressed they then turned towards Malcolm that was now looking like a deflated balloon, "so what do we have here, some real showers of shite by the looks of it Roger what do you think" Roger walked towards the men swinging the bat while fixated on Malcolm "so you don't like us black bastards and think its ok to bully a little girl, well I think it's time we taught you some manners and respect" as he swung the bat and cracked it across Malcolm's shoulders, Tyrone turned his attention to Robert who was already backing up the grass with his hands up in surrender, no way was he getting involved with this "it weren't me it was him" Malcolm already on his knees was clasping his shoulder which he knew was broken and shot Robert a look of venom "you cu" before he could finish off the sentence

9

Tyrone and Roger pounced and gave him a good old fashion kicking, laughing as Tyrone booted him so hard Malcom lifted off the grass.

When they finished Roger flashed everyone a bright smile he hadn't even broke a sweat, looking at Robert "now fuck off and take this silly mug with you, and by the way don't ever come back on this estate again you hear me now boy!" they nodded and pulled a battered bloody Malcolm of the grass, Tyrone picked up the discarded bats and turned to see little Ronnie standing there watching the whole thing with her hands on her hips she looked at Tyrone "no one will ever hurt my little Terry I will kill them" her eyes were sparkling blue full of emotion, he couldn't look away he was mesmerised, she looked up at him, he just nodded he didn't understand what he was feeling but he knew what ever happened they were bonded by today and he made a pact to himself that he would always protect this girl with the blue eyes and blond hair with his life.

At 14 years of age Tyrone was what Sue referred to as a lump the sheer size of him already filled the doorframe he definitely took after his father and already looked older than his years, he held out his hand and Ronnie without hesitation took it for some reason that she didn't understand she felt safe with him "come on let's see what mum has knocked us up for dinner" the skin heads were quickly forgotten as they walked down the grass back to Sues, Kelly couldn't believe her eyes! She watched them walk back Tyrone was a big lump of a boy next to little Ronnie but for some reason they just seem to fit, my god wait till I tell mum and everyone at school tomorrow! she run off back to her house knowing the street would be alive with tonight's action being discussed by all!

Upstairs Nancy who was happily swaying around the flat drinking a very large vodka and Coke Ronnie was long forgotten, her daughter meanwhile, was downstairs, in her element, everyone was happy sitting together around Sues old scrubbed pine table chattering at all at once Ronnie looked around her and truly understood what it felt like to belong, and at that very same moment Sue looked at her little family and her heart swelled with pride, little did they realise that in years to come, Ronnie would become a part of the family in every way.

Chapter two

Nancy was swaying to the beat of her favourite Lionel Richie track on the radio she knew tonight was important for Billy and she wanted to make sure she made the right impression, She was dressed to kill her makeup was faultless she knew she looked good, looking at herself in the mirror her sparkling blue eyes were heavily lined and drew you to her she knew they were her best feature, her raven black hair fell to her shoulders in shiny waves, she was the total opposite of her daughter she had dark, olive skinned to Ronnie's fair hair, pale skin and freckles the only thing that they shared was the eyes. Nancy had never met the Donnelley's but knew they were heavy duty, real faces and whatever they wanted with Billy it certainly would be interesting, compared to them Billy was the small fish swimming in their large pond, Billy run brasses and brothels, he made his money by selling tits and arse and cocaine, he garnered respect and loyalty in the workforce by slapping and cutting women. Billy was a spiteful little shit and ruled his little workforce with an iron rod, she had heard the Donnelley's had worked their way up and were well-liked by a lot of people on the manner, they had earnt their respect from the ground up, they were known to be firm, merciless, but fair, their reputation was solid. Nancy mused and wondered what they would want with Billy, it must be a real earner, she hoped that the days of her having to take a quick fumble up a cold wall in a dark alleyway were well and truly numbered.

While Nancy waited on Billy and the Donnelley's, Adam and Stevie Donnelly were making their way across the streets of east London to Bethnal Green, Stevie as always thinking of his stomach turn to Adam and said any chance we can stop of at Pelliches I'm Hank Marvin And I want to line my stomach before we get to Billy's birds house, Adam laughed "listen Steve we need to cut this deal tonight so save your stomach and let's get down to business, will go out and eat later you know the Dallas does a lovely bit of steak and has a lock in, it's just around the corner from Billy's birds gaff" Stevie laughed "fair point bruv anyway what's the crack? why Billy? I don't even like him he's a spiteful bastard to his women and that don't sit well with me, you don't need to beat or mark up a woman to keep her in line" Adam nodded in agreement "I know, but we need his connections there is not a man he don't know in the smoke that ain't worth knowing and I want to put cocaine through he's brothels and spread it amongst

11

our boys and network of bars and clubs and more importantly I want his northern network, this deal is a serious feather in our cap a proper fucking earner so be nice and on your best behaviour please", Stevie being the more fiery one laughed and threw his hands up "scouts honour bruv but if he gets lairy I can't make no promises" Stevie chuckled as he threw the car around the corner like a rally driver "this jag is a tasty motor bruv it handles the corner real nice" "well take it easy I would like this one to last a bit longer then the last one" Stevie had a reputation for driving like the devil was on his tail and had killed a few engines already.

Stevie And Adam Donnelly come from seriously naughty family their mother Puna gave birth to 13 children in quick succession, they were all very close knit, and had the blood of the East End running through their veins, the rules of the pavement were drummed into them at an early age. As they rose steadily amongst the ranks, they were quickly respected by their peers for not only their business acumen but for also being very handy to the point of cold blooded ruthless. Their businesses ranged from scrap yards to pubs, clubs, Casinos, restaurants and local bookie's, they loved the hunt of the next deal we're very handy with a shooter and was always seemed to be one step ahead of the law , they didn't think they were untouchable, they happily greased more palms then a second hand fortune teller, keeping the filth and locals sweet was a part and parcel of life and kept them from having their collars felt, to the Donnelly's buying information was like buying bread and milk from the local corner shop they had eyes and ears everywhere and they knew the next stop was taking over the brothels that belonged to Billy. The key to their success was placing a member of family into each business, there were no outsiders at the head of any of their vast network thus they never had any internal problems, the family was close knit and it showed you fucked with one you had thirteen of them coming down on your head like a ton of bricks. Everyone knew the score Adam was the think tank, the brains and always came up with the ideas and Stevie the silver-tongued devil that could sell it.

Even though the men and women of the family made money hand over fist they stayed true to their roots, looked after their own, made sure everyone had a piece of action, they brought their childhood friends up with them, loyalty was everything, their word was law on the streets of east London, if any action took part on their manor it had to be ok'd by the boys and they took a slice, a cut it was always given with no resentment as they were not greedy, it was given out of respect, they had the new school in their sons and they were the old school the combination of both was a winner.

As they were making their way across to the meet, Billy was already at the flat with Nancy, "girl you look the bollocks you're going to knock them dead" Nancy smiled and drunk the last dregs of vodka that was in her glass steady on Nancy she told herself, try and keep it together because for some reason she felt nervous maybe it was because this was the unknown and she didn't want to fuck it up, she turned to

Billy and flashed her million dollar smile "I won't let you down Bill" he slapped her ass playfully " I know you won't because you know what will happen if you do" she nodded uneasily "now be a good girl and go fix me a drink sweetheart, a large one" As she started to pour a large measure into his glass there was a knock at door, Billy jumped up flustered he ran to answer it, Nancy was shocked she had never seen Billy act so nervously, as he opened the door Nancy knew why, the sheer size of the brothers filled her door frame, as they walked in their sheer presence filled the room, fuck me these are dangerous men, they had that aura of authority that told you they were the guvnors, as she took in the sheer size of them Nancy locked eyes with Adam, the connection between them was immediate, electric, Nancy's mouth went dry her whole body shook, she could not tear her eyes away, she drank him in with her eyes. Adam also looked at Nancy like he had been struck with lightning, he was transfixed, oh shit I'm in trouble here, for some unexplainable reason he could not break the stare that was going on between them, it was like a magnet was trying to pull him closer towards her, he felt like all of the air was punched from his body and someone had reached within him and had a tight grip on his heart, what the fuck is happening to me pull yourself together you going to fuck this up, Stevie sensing that something wasn't right looked across at his brother and try to break the tangible tension that was now in the air, on cue he smiled and kissed Nancy on the cheek, "hello sweetheart I'm Steven this is my brother Adam were spitting feathers here any chance of a drink" he smiled and gave her a saucy wink, Nancy blushed a deep crimson and pulled her eyes away from Adam and managed to reply huskily "I've got scotch vodka and beers what's your poison" She snuck a look at Adam again as she asked the question, Stevie smiled to himself trying not to laugh as he thought oh shit I can see the deal going up in flames. He looked across at Billy and realised he was oblivious thank god let's see if we can salvage this before it truly goes south "I'll have a scotch sweetheart and Adam will have a beer, Billy what you having" "no you're alright mate my Nancy just poured me one" "Right let's get down to business Nancy excuse yourself and let us boys have a chat" Nancy looked across at Billy and nodded she couldn't even speak, she was rendered speechless. What is going on? she had never felt anything like it in her life, this lump of a man had awoken something within her and it had blown her apart in seconds, her feelings were so scattered she couldn't even get out of that room quick enough.

As Stevie was outlining the plan for a Coke distribution telling him the cut that Billy would earn Adam kept looking at the door he knew he was in trouble, but he didn't care, feelings like this only ever happened once or twice if you're lucky in your life, he had to see her and he was going to make sure he did, it was more than just attraction that much he was sure of. As his brother was reeling Billy in on the deal he smiled warily to himself money always made greedy fuckers act like a rat up a drain pipe, little did Billy know that within weeks of him networking the Coke through his men they would taking over his houses and the running of his girls, it would just be another add to their ever expanding business and seeing as no one liked Billy it would not ruffle any feathers in fact a lot of the working girls would probably be breathing a sigh of relief. Adam was the thinker and Stevie was the smooth salesman he made the deal sound so good, no one ever turned them down, Adam tore his eyes away from the door and watched Stevie reeling Billy in, he smiled as he watched them talking the finer details, not that it mattered Billy would get a serious wedge to walk away from it all, we would be fair, and he was sure that Billy would take the money to save face, his thoughts were interrupted when Stevie said "So what do you think Bill sound like a plan?" "sure does mate I think we can go into business together and make a killing" Stevie chuckled "making a killing is right boy", he reached across the table and shook Billy's hand, smiling magnanimously thinking mate you have no idea, "now we got that little bit of business out the way me and my brother have got a few other irons in the fire so to speak, so we're going to love you and leave you" Adam looked at Stevie and said "Bill why don't you and your Nancy come with us to the Dallas steakhouse they have some good music on tonight, its proper lively and you know they do a lock in, let's have a drink and seal the deal" Stevie looked across at Adam his eyebrows raised, Adam was not one to mix business with pleasure, he didn't know what was going on with his little brother he was acting like a horny teenager he shook his head wearily, Billy puffed his chest out with pride being seen with these two men would be all round the streets by the end of the night, he shouted up to Nancy "get your coat on girl we are off out" Nancy jumped up from the end of the bed and pulled her best coat out of the wardrobe, this coat was only used on a serious special occasion, she had bought it from Rita the shop lifter for a song, she slipped it on and walked from the bedroom it was a thick silver fox coat with luxurious pelts its white fur was a startling contrast to her black Raven hair she had sprayed herself liberally with her favourite perfume and slowly walk down the stairs. All three men looked up as she walked down, billy threw his arm round her shoulders, "she's a stunner isn't she" Billy was totally oblivious to the atmosphere in the room, Adam and Nancy locked eyes and he took a deep breath his eyes never leaving hers "she sure is" his heart was pounding.

"Come on Billy we will take my car" Stevie said dryly looking at the two idiots behind him, still looking like a pair lovesick puppy's "They do a lovely steak here boy I'm hank Marvin so let's go" As they walked towards the car, Nancy's brain was working nine to the dozen I don't know what to do, I don't know how to act. I can't even hide it. They all jumped in Stevie's Jag and set off, it felt like the longest ten minutes of Nancy's life, Billy was chattering on, Nancy could tell he had obviously snuck a few cheeky lines in when no one was looking as he was going full pelt trying to impress the two big men that sat in the front, Billy was acting like a right mug it was embarrassing, Nancy forced herself to look out of the window so she didn't focus on the silhouette of the body in front of her, at the same time Adam could feel her eyes burning into the back of his head and it took every inch of will power not to turn round and look at her.

As everyone got out of the car Stevie pulled Adam back and whispered in his ear "what the fuck is going on your acting like a dog on heat, pull yourself together and remember the deal is what's important here and the fact but you're bloody married" Adam looked Stevie in the face "twenty years of a loveless marriage with no kids, I don't know what's going on with me but I'm telling you this that woman has shook me to my core, I know she's a brass but something has happened between us, call it a spark, call it whatever you want but I need to know as it's never happened to me before bruv" Stevie look at his brother and could see his eyes blazing, he put his arm around his shoulders "well if it isn't them prize knockers putting you into a trance I suppose you going to have to find out what it is" he laughed at Adams face "you look like you've been struck by lightning" Stevie's heart was heavy, deep down he knew that Debbie was a heartless bitch, the home was loveless and it showed. Adam had stayed by her side for twenty years because that was how they was raised, respect loyalty and honour, it was one of the reasons they were so highly regarded on street, everything they stood for on the pavement also stood as a rule in their homes, even if that women was a bitter pill, she had endured a couple of miscarriages and Adam being of the old school, he would not leave her it just wasn't in him, of course he had a few one night stands and a regular bird here and there who could blame him with that sour faced fucker. Stevie thought she needs aiming headfirst out of the door but kept that little nugget to himself "come on boy let's get you a steak because you look hungry for something" they laughed as they walked in side by side.

 As the brothers walked in the door, Antonio spotted them and rushed to greet them, he shook their hands warmly "my friends, Adam, Stevie I haven't seen you in a long time, come I've got a table ready let me look after you" Billy and Nancy were at the bar and Stevie waved them over, as they walked behind the brothers heads were turning in the restaurant, many nodded or shook their hand in acknowledgement, Billy feeling the buzz that was in the air looked at the men and realised this is who he wanted to be, but deep down knew in his heart that he would never have the respect or presence that they had on the street, embarrassed he looked across at Nancy and saw her flushed face and felt a spark of jealousy rush through his body he knew he would never compare to the two men that in front of him and it hurt, he tugged hard on Nancy's arm digging his fingers into her and sneered at her spitefully "keep your legs crossed bitch I can smell you from here your like a dog on heat" Nancy's eyes widened in shock, she looked at him and with as much dignity as she could muster she smiled and said sweetly "are you suffering from a bit of little man syndrome if you are don't put your shit on me, I'm just here for the ride sweetheart remember" He looked at her shocked that she had the balls to answer him back "just remember you're here with me, keep your mouth shut and look pretty or you'll be back down commercial street selling your arse quicker than your feet can touch the ground" as this little fracas was playing out Adam and Stevie was already seated, Adam was watching Nancy's face change and could see the spiteful look on Billy's face, keeping his face neutral he smiled as they walked towards the table and poured them both of glass of wine courtesy of Antonio. Nancy picked up her glass and sipped the cold crisp wine while keeping her eyes firmly down looking at the tablecloth, it was the only way to stop herself looking at Adam, Stevie sensing the atmosphere around the table cleared his throat and said "the food here is pukka let's order" and rubbed his hands together.

As the food started coming to the table Nancy kept quiet and concentrated on cutting and eating small pieces of steak it was the only way she could control herself, Adam was staring at her thinking I even like the way she chews, Stevie knowing the score started a conversation up with Billy so Adam could have a crack at the girl, he soon realised billy was a right mug as he droned on about a complete load of bullshit, his jaw swinging told him he was off his face, Stevie was doing everything in his power to stop his eyes from glazing over, he glanced at Adam and thought you owe me big time "so Nancy tell me a little bit about yourself where are your from, and how long have you been with that wally" Nancy stopped chewing and took a slow sip of her wine savouring the flavour and thought her goes nothing, no point in sugar coating it, for some reason she knew this man commanded nothing but the complete truth, she just couldn't lie to him, she looked at him and shrugged "there's not much to say you know who I am, you know what I am, and where I'm from don't really matter I don't apologise for who I am either, I've been with Billy a couple of weeks and it's not exactly a match made in heaven" she smiled unsure of herself as she felt like she was in uncharted territory, she looked around and realised Billy was still in deep conversation with Steve, "you make me feel uncomfortable" she whispered to Adam "I'm a grown woman and I don't know what to say to you" Adam laughed "right back at ya girl I feel like a randy schoolboy" she laughed relieved that it wasn't just her imagination.

The background music of the steakhouse was gradually getting louder, and as the tables were clearing, people started to get up and dance Adam shouted to Billy above the din "Bill do you mind if I have a dance with your Nancy" Billy put his hand up and waved him away "no problem" as he was heavily engrossed with Stevie who was starting to look like he had all but lost the will to live. Adam held his hand out, Nancy took a deep breath and put her hand in his the feeling that hit her was like a jolt that run straight through her body, she walked shakily to the dance floor "I don't believe this she laughed this is my favourite song" as Lionel Richie started blaring out of the speakers, Adam laughed "is it come on then girl let's cut some shapes" Nancy roared with laughter and got caught up in the moment "come on then show me what you're made of" they both got lost to the music drinking each other in with their eyes, laughing as they threw out their best moves! As they were dancing she knew this was the perfect moment, she slipped him a napkin with her phone number on it, Adam quickly folded it into his pocket not missing a beat keeping his face neutral he pulled her hand and they made their way back from the dance floor. Nancy sat down fanning her face Billy smiled at her "you alright babe" already forgetting the insults of earlier on she smiled sweetly while her heart was pumping in her chest "yes Bill all good darling" inside she wanted to scream, she was stepping into the unknown and it felt dangerously good.

.

Adam was sitting in a portacabin in the back of Canning town for three days he had looked at the phone number written on the napkin, for some reason he couldn't explain this girl Nancy had got right under his skin, he was trying to play it cool, not trying be too eager I'll give it a few days and then I'll ring her and take her for a drink and see how it all plays out, that's what he had told himself the night they pulled away from the Dallas, Stevie had moaned all the way home you would think he had took a bullet the way he was carrying on! He sipped on his glass of single malt and picked up the phone, it it's all or nothing, he dialled the number and after a few rings Nancy's deep distinctive gravelly voice answered the phone, fucking hell even her phone voice was sexy "hello darling it's Adam can you talk?" Nancy smiled down the phone "I'm alone, how are you? I was thinking about you and the phone rang" he started to feel that familiar ache again, the past three days had been torture not seeing her "do you fancy coming out for a drink and a bit of dinner" "where are you thinking" Nancy smiled "you know it has to be off the manner because of Billy" " fuck Billy" Adam laughed "you don't have to worry about him" she could feel the pull of him, the attraction was strong "ok let me know when and we'll go for it" taking a deep pull on her cigarette "I can't wait to see you" Adam laughed "that feeling is definitely mutual" he told Nancy about a nice little restaurant in the back of Brentwood, it was discreet and the food was good "I'll pick you up around eight" she smiled "see you at eight them" she put the phone gently back onto the cradle, it's on! she knew wherever this led she was in for the ride, she was a firm believer when life through your curveball you ran with it and for Adam she was willing to do all the running.

Nancy took extra care getting ready she chose a red silk blouse that was unbuttoned, showing a sexy hint of cleavage and a fitted black leather pencil skirt, black silk stockings and her best heeled pumps, she had a beautiful wardrobe full of clothes she had bought off the local shoplifters in the hope that one day she would get to wear them, she was now so glad she had, she looked amazing no one would ever know what she did for a living in this get up that she was sure of. Nancy had already sent Ronnie downstairs to Sue and slipped Sue a tenner and asked her to keep an eye on her for the night, Sue looked at Nancy curiously as Nancy's face was flushed and she couldn't meet her gaze, she kept her own counsel as she know nothing stayed a secret for long, the truth always outs, she smiled at Nancy as she took the tenner thinking this is going to be interesting, "no problem sweetheart your little one is no bother at all" Nancy felt fear trickle down her spine for the first time in a long time she was nervous and scared, she didn't want to fuck this up and she didn't want Billy to find out, he was one spiteful bastard and would go mental, but Nancy being the girl she was, didn't give a rats ass, pushing the fear aside, she was attracted to danger like a moth to the flame .

Nancy appraised herself critically in a mirror she looked completely different and that was what she wanted sexy but classy understated and miles away from the street hustler that she was, she sprayed herself liberally on the wrists and ankles and breasts with Anais Anais and shook her hair out, her blue eyes were sparkling with excitement, looking at the mirror finally nodding with approval, "I'm ready" she took a black clutch bag and walked downstairs and poured herself a stiff drink to steady her nerves as she waited for Adam .

Adam was freshly shaved and had a handmaid shirt open at the neck his gold Rolex peeking out from the cuff, he looked like what he was, discreet and understated he didn't have to flaunt the wealth. As he drove across Bethnal Green, he thought how this was this going to play out, obviously this wasn't the first time but he had a played away from home, with the wife he had it wasn't surprising! but this felt different. Adam looked every inch of what he was, a dangerous man, a face. Thinking of Nancy had made Adam feel like a randy schoolboy, Stevie had taken the piss out of him all afternoon, it had been a long time since Stevie had seen Adam like this all worked up over something else other than work, it was good to him come to life, the man was obsessed with grafting. As Adam pulled up outside Nancy's block and jumped out of his car, Sue's eyes widened in shock well stone the crows no wonder Nancy was keeping this one under her hat, she tried to make it not look too obvious that she was staring but Adam caught her eye and tipped Sue a saucy wink "alright girl how's your boys" Sue's mouth opened, she nodded as for once nothing came out of her mouth, Adam chuckled to himself "anytime your Tyrone wants to earn a few quid you send him over to me he is a good lad I will keep a watch over him" Sue was speechless he only knew her Tyrone! Adam walked in the block as Sue sat there, she could not believe it, bloody hell! Adam Donnelly! I don't even think I want to tell anybody about this, Billy Simpson was a spiteful bastard and if he found out God only knows what he do to Nancy's face, he was known for cutting brasses the spiteful bastard, no I will keep stoom, mum is definitely the word, Sue sipped her brandy waiting in anticipation, Adam run up the stairs and knocked on Nancy's door and laughed as she opened it, they both eyed each other up hungrily "bloody el girl you're a knockout", Nancy laughed and blushed and with that deep sexy voice she sent tingles up his spine as she replied "you're not too bad yourself" she could feel the heat rising inside her, Adam looked at Nancy like he literally wanted to eat her alive" you hungry" she smiled "I'm famished" he swallowed slowly putting his hand out "come on girl let's get this party started"

As they walked out of the block and across to Adams car Sue could not believe what was unfolding in front of her Nancy looked the absolute business, she watched as Adam opened her door and Nancy sat in the car, Nancy kept her eyes forward too scared to look anywhere but ahead in case someone locked eyes with her she knew she was playing with fire but she didn't give a damn.

Adam started the car and the radio sprung to life, low in the background, he drove through Bethnal Green and slowly onto the Roman road he made small talk sensing she was a little shy "so tell me what the fuck are you doing with a fella like Billy Simpson" "he's a mate" she smiled "I was going to work in one of his houses" Adam looked across at her "you're better than that, you sell yourself too short you should be running the houses not lying down in one of them" Nancy didn't know what to say as he turned onto the A12 they drove past Romford, Nancy noticed that the area was less built up and the houses were obviously worth a lot of money "I've never been out this far before" she looked at him and smiled, Adam looked back at her "my house is only down the road in Chigwell I don't go there very often I stay in one of my flats in Wapping it's more suitable for me to remain close to our business interests, look I'm going to be honest with you I'm married, don't judge me, just hear me out, my marriage is dead it has been for a long time, my wife is a devout Catholic and it'll be a cold day in hell before she gives me a divorce she likes the idea of us being shackled together" Nancy was shocked with his honesty "have you got any kids" he shook his head "no" Adam gripped the steering wheel showing the whites of his knuckles "she had a couple of miscarriages and everything changed, she became distant very bitter and jealous of the relationship I had with my family, I go back a couple times a week but it's a charade the house suffocates me, it's not a home there's nothing left for me there, what about you Nancy have you ever been married" she looked at him and laughed "I'm not the marrying type, I've never been married but I have a little girl called Ronnie she's 11 the father was never on the scene in fact I don't know who he was she's a good girl and she's coped well with the fact that her mother is a prostitute I've always been very honest with her" Adam looked at her shocked "I didn't know you had a daughter" Nancy laughed "well seeing as you've only known me a week I'm sure there's a lot we don't know about each other" as they drove through Brentwood Adam said "were nearly there, I know it's a bit of a drive but trust me the food is worth it" They pulled off the main road onto a long shingle drive and drove up to a large country house "wow this is a restaurant?" Nancy was impressed "yeah it does weddings, special occasions and all of the food is locally sourced, organic" she was taken aback "how do you know so much about this place, are you a regular?" as he opened the door to help her out onto the gravel "no babe I own it" Nancy opened her mouth and shut it well not much I can say to that. She tucked her hand through his arm and they walked up the steps together to the entrance Adam was greeted warmly by the maître D and staff and was shown to a beautifully set table that overlooked the back of the restaurant gardens it was beautifully manicured and had a large lake, Nancy looked around "Adam where's all the customers?" "just me and you tonight baby I hope you don't mind I wanted to get to know you, no noise, no interruptions" Nancy felt like her legs were going to give out from under her, Adam pulled out her chair and she sat down gratefully, she watched him walk with the confidence only an accomplished man would have, she smiled oh yes he had the swagger all right, she could not keep her eyes off of him, how was she going to get through this meal? she could feel the heat rising between her legs and travelling up her stomach making her blush "lets order some wine" Adam looked across at her she replied "something cool" looking at her chest he laughed I don't know how I'm going to keep my hands off of you, "Then don't" she replied his breath quickened "fuck sake Nance let's order this dinner quick" he could feel himself slowly stiffening and took a deep breath calm down this isn't your first rodeo enjoy this mate you're acting like a lovesick teenager, maybe it wasn't a good idea to bring her here, "shall I order for both of us now?" she nodded at him "yes surprise me" out of nowhere Richard took the order and he disappeared as fast as he arrived the table was set beautifully, candles, Crisp white tablecloth, sparkling crystal and a beautiful bowl of freshly cut peonies lightly fragranced the divide between them Nancy looked around, "this place is amazing you must be so proud of what you've accomplished" he leaned back in his chair "I love it here this is my baby, Stevie didn't understand the vision I had for his place but I know that we could make this something special and we have" she smiled "you did good" she raised her glass to him, and took a sip of the delicious wine.

As each course was placed on the table the conversation between them was effortless, funny and deep all at the same time they found that they had a lot of things in common, Adam was shocked "still waters run deep with you you're more than a pretty face girl" Nancy looked at him "right back at you" and he laughed, the meal was drawing to an end, and she felt a shift in the atmosphere "well" Adam looked at her the night is still young do you fancy going out for a little nightcap? Nancy looked directly at him "no Adam I want you to take me home to your flat" Adams mouth went dry "your wish is my command" he got up from his seat and pulled back the chair for Nancy he held his handout "Are you sure about this?" Nancy placed her hand in his and laughed "what do you think" and they were off.

Nancy couldn't tell you how long it took to get from Brentwood to Wapping but the way Adam drove she was sure he broke the land speed record as she pulled up outside his flat she was surprise to see one of the old warehouse conversions "I've heard about these" "yeah it's it up and coming area we bought a lot of property along the docks and Wapping, in years to come you mark my words it's going to be worth a fortune" she had no doubt "you have your fingers in many pies don't you" he looked at her and winked "sweetheart you have no idea" as they got into the lift it took every ounce self-control to keep their hands off of each other, Adam looked at Nancy and could feel his erection growing she looked up at him, directly into his eyes her face was flushed she muttered "when is this door going to bloody open" "fuck this" Adam replied as he grabbed Nancy around the waist and pulled her towards him he she moaned as he started to kiss her deeply sliding his tongue into her mouth the smell of her intoxicated him I have never wanted anyone like I want this woman right now, as he thought it the lift door opened and he stepped back, they were both panting looking at each other "come on we here" he opened the door to the flat.

Nancy took in the open plan kitchen and living room with windows going across the expanse of the wall with a phenomenal view of the River Thames and Tower of London, before Nancy could even speak Adam scooped her up into his arms, her skirt had hitched around her waist as she wrapped her legs around his waist, they started to deeply kiss each other, Nancy licked his bottom lip, he tasted off scotch, she probed his mouth with her tongue not wanting to come up for air, Adam carried Nancy into the bedroom and placed her gently on the floor by the bed, he looked down at her savouring the look in her eyes, she reached over and started undoing the buttons of his shirt slowly, whatever happens she thought, I'll never forget this as long as I live, he started to unbuckle his belt and kicked off his shoes, she lifted her blouse over her head, he stared at her shaking his head drinking in women in front of him she had worn an intricate lace Basque and it took every inch of self-control not to rip it off her body, he looked up and down at her appraisingly, fuck me she's even wearing stockings, that was his undoing he stripped the rest of his clothes off kissing her slowly, stroking her breasts as she went to remove her underwear he put his hand up "no let me do it" he laid her on the bed and peeled her lingerie slowly off her, leaving trails of kisses over her breasts trailing down to her stomach towards her legs gently licking her until she spread her legs apart, she couldn't wait no more she could feel herself already building up, she licked her hand and reached towards his manhood slowly caressing him pulling his skin back as he jolted with the sensations she started to build up a rhythm, he looked at her "let me fuck you" His words were her undoing, she was dripping with want for this man, he was now directly above her holding himself up looking into her eyes like he had never seen such a women, she arched her pelvis and he entered her with one deep thrust, they both groaned together as he steadily started to thrust deeply into her, Nancy wrapped her legs around his body and pulled his face towards hers biting his lip, kissing him deeply she had never felt so aroused in her life she was dripping with excitement and could feel the build-up in her body, please not yet she told herself she could feel he's hot manhood thickening as he was pushing deeper into her "harder" she panted "I want all of you" he looked into her eyes pushing into her deeper, she could feel herself start letting go and begun to shudder as she started to come, he pushed one final deep thrust and finally felt himself release into her, they were both throbbing. Adam was dazed, as Nancy looked up at him he bent down and gently kissed her lips looking at her "I've never felt like this with anyone" she knew he was telling her the truth, because she felt the same, she felt a tear escape down the side of her face and he wiped it with his thumb looking at her questioningly and she replied simply "neither have I".

For three days they didn't leave the flat there was either in the bed, or making love in the shower, or sitting at the table eating take away drinking wine, laughing and talking, Adam looked over at Nancy wearing one of his shirts and a pair of his boxers, not even a scrap of makeup, Adam felt the pull of the sexy woman that was sitting opposite him, he had fallen for her and had fallen hard. The family couldn't believe that Adam had put Stevie in charge of the business it was unheard of, the gossip mill was running on overdrive, who was Adam Donnelly shacked up with? that's what everyone wanted to know he knew he was going to get roasted by the brothers but it would be in good humour, they were shocked as Adam was never away from his desk. Nancy looked across at her lover and also knew she was hopelessly in love with him, Ronnie was forgotten about, she knew Sue would look after her, all that mattered was this man in front of her right now he consumed her with a passion she never knew she had, she felt like a flower that finally was seeing some sunlight, she had opened up her petals and let this beautiful man in, everything was about to change.

"Listen Adam I have to go home I'm wearing your boxers and shirts I have to get back to normality it's been five days now I have to go home!" he looked at her and laughed "I suppose you're right but you do realise everything's going to be up in the air, the next few days are going to be heavy, I'm going to have a word with Billy he won't be coming to your flat no more and you won't be working no more if you want to run a couple of houses and earn some bunce or run one of the Strip clubs I will put you in one, I know it's early days Nancy but I can't let you go" Nancy looked up at Adam and nodded she felt the pull of him she knew he was married and she didn't care, she would have him anyway she could get him. She jumped up on the cool marble work top and looked at him, he knew that look, he smiled slowly and sauntered towards her he started slowly unbuttoning the shirt she was wearing "you look good in this" as he cupped her breast rubbing his thumb over her nipple in slow circles, with the other hand he undid the buttons on his jeans and pulled he's already erect penis out of his boxers, he placed his hand into the small of back and pulled her towards him, with one deep thrust he entered her, Nancy let out a deep sigh, it all felt so right, Adam was exited to feel she was already wet, he started to push into her deep and fast, she moaned louder with excitement and laid back on the counter top arching her back in pleasure as Adam ran his hands down her body and breasts and placed his hands on her hips pushing himself into her deeper, she wrapped her legs around his body, it was a hot deep fast fuck, he could already feel her tightening around him and it made him throb, she was an aphrodisiac to him he could fill himself expanding inside her, he thrusted faster and could feel her start to quiver "I'm going to come" she looked into his eyes unashamed no one had ever made her feel like this, with that she fell to 1000 pieces. Adam let out a deep grunt and felt the release he needed, they orgasmed together, clinging to each other, neither could believe how mind blowing they were together.

As their breathing slowed down and they started to come back down to earth, they smiled, both high on each other, Adam pulled himself out of Nancy gently and picked her up off the work top, placing her gently on the floor he held out his hand and took her into their walk in shower, he stripped off and they walked into together both smiling at each other like a pair of love sick teenagers, as they washed each other's backs and bodies, both were aware that something deep was happening

22

between them. As they got dried and started to get dressed, they already had the air of familiarity around them "come on girl back to reality we go" she smiled at him Adam felt the familiar ache the only she could do to him. They left the flat and jumped into the car, as they were driving back to Bethnal Green Adam looked at Nancy "I'd like to meet your daughter Ronnie I'm not going nowhere you know that don't you" she held his hand over the gear stick and smiled "I can't believe this is happening to me" she couldn't even say the words out loud I love you Adam she didn't dare, outside the flat Sue was sitting dog eye, she knew she had to come back sooner or later but nearly four days, even on Nancy's standard was sailing close to the wind, she shook her head bloody hell that girl was taking a right liberty. As Sue thought it, Adam turned into the close and pulled up outside the flats, she watched Adam jump out of the car and open the door for Nancy and looked at their faces her eyes widened at what she saw, oh my God there in love, Adam walked over to Sue and tucked a ton in her hand, "sorry I kept Nancy away but we needed to get to know each other" and with a cheeky wink he turned to Nancy and kissed her deeply "I will see you later ok babe" all Nancy could do was nod she didn't know what to say she stood at the side of the pavement as he drove off and then turned to face Sue "before you say anything you better pour me a large glass of whatever you have got in that house" Sue jumped up like someone had lit a match under her all her anger was forgotten this was the gossip of the century!

Chapter three

Nancy sat down heavily into the chair and rested her arms on Sues pine table the irony was not lost on her; this table had become the local confessional and Sue was the priest. "I'm sorry I left Ronnie with you for so long it just went mental" Sue waved her hand "let's forget about that, tell me everything" her eyes like saucers, "Billy has been going mad I hid Ronnie upstairs when he was outside your flat What are you going to do?" Nancy drained the glass in one gulp and refilled before answering "Billy is done Adam will take care of him I am with Adam now" she tried to hide the smile off her face, "I can't believe this is happening to me I've fallen for him hard" her hands shaking as she refilled the glass, love was a mystery to her, "does he feel the same way?" "yeah I think he does, isn't that crazy Adam Donnelly had fallen for a brass" Nancy shook her head "what am I going to do?" Sue leaned across the table and grabbed Nancy's hand "you're going to roll with it babe that's what you're going to do, it's about time you had a bit of luck in your life now Ronnie isn't due home from school yet for at least a couple of hours, go and put your head down because honestly you looked fucked!" Nancy laughed as it was true, reaching into her bag she peeled two £50 pound notes from a thick wad of money that Adam had given her, she had to pinch herself she had never seen that amount of money in her life she handed it to Sue "thanks Sue this is for all the times I have taken the piss you have always watched over my Ronnie and I wanted to show that I appreciate what you do for her" Sue felt herself welling up "you don't know how handy this money is for me right now I am on my ass you and Adam just got me out of a right tight spot girl you've literally just saved my bacon" they laughed as they held hands and looked across at each other smiling, that day a friendship was made that would last to the end of their lives.

Adam drove the Jag through the city as if he was on auto pilot, it was time to get back to work he smiled wearily at himself in the rear-view mirror he was happy and it showed, fucking hell I'm going to be roasted by the family, but he didn't care he had a feeling Nancy was more than a passing fling and was willing to face the Spanish inquisition from the firm. As made his way to one of the clubs they owned in Soho he parked up outside and nodded acknowledgment to the doorman and girls as he walked through the main floor, as he approached the bar Mandy poured him a large scotch and pushed it over to him, "alright Adam, we haven't seen you for a few days, your looking well" she appraised him from head to toe fluttering her false eyelashes at him, Adam chuckled "so I take it I'm the topic of conversation" "well put it this way there's not many people that don't know" Adam frowned hoping that he could have kept it quiet for a little longer as he still had to deal with Billy, he drank his whiskey in a swift gulp and placed the glass back down on the bar, "thanks mand I needed that" Adam walked upstairs to the main offices where all they main graft was done, Stevie preferred the yards but Adam liked the offices up west, when people first come through the doors they were often shocked at how light and airy it was, it was a total contrast to the club that was dark wood, smoky mirrors and deep rich colours, the bar was a place you could remain anonymous in the dark corners and private seating areas, it was members only club and was a haunt for politicians, actors and the upper class, the waiting list was long, and thus made the club even more sought after, you knew you were among the elite when you had the little black and gold card in your wallet the yearly fees were eye watering, and were often paid well in advance. Within the silk clad walls, the club held all the secrets of its clientele, and its patrons were comfortable in the knowledge knowing what was said and done in the club stayed there.

Adam walked into the conference room and looked at the large group of seriously naughty men that were gathered there, "hello mate" he stopped and shook hands as he walked to the head of the large table, he put his hands up " please take a seat let's get down to business" as the men took their seats he looked around the table, he was surrounded by the best team that London had to offer, black and white sat shoulder to shoulder, he had the heavy's, the drugs, the houses, the yards and clubs every business had someone from his network sitting at the helm and they were all here looking at him, "before I start let me get something of my chest, as I can see the look in your eyes you bunch of nosey fuckers have already got wind that I have been away for a few days with a friend shall we say, now as your all aware this women has a past and to be honest I don't give a fuck, but if anyone has anything to say spit it out now because if I ever hear anything that one of you have been talking beyond this room I won't be a happy bunny" as he looked around the room you could hear a pin drop, Daniel cleared his throat, "Adam listen brother I feel you yeah, my mum was a working girl the same yeah, women have to do what they have to do to survive especially when they have mouths to feed, it's all good brother, I like Nancy she is a total rocket brother and I speak for all of us, we wish you well fella" Adam looked around the room and see the men relax and laughed "I'm not saying its loves young dream but while she is with me she is treated with respect" all the men nodded in agreement, they understood the coo and respected Adam for bringing it up. "Now we have that out the way first point of business is Billy we already have garnered the contacts we need to shift the coke through his clubs and houses, and we have the northern pipeline open, but obviously we are going to have to move fast" Adam got up and poured himself a glass of whiskey from the well-stocked bar, "now hold tight boys this is how were going to play this one out" As he sat down he pulled each part of the firm into the plan and explained to them how he wanted the work handled, Stevie sat back and watched his brother at work, thinking to himself, this boy is like a fucking magician the stunts he pulls were seriously another level, he was pulled from his thoughts when Adam said "Stevie I want Billy in this office by the end of the day I'm going to pay him off, men you have people in mind that can take over his places, if any of Billy's people are worth keeping onside good, keep them if not I want them outed by the end of the day and your people in place to take over so we are not losing any money, I know its quick but that's why your sitting here with me you're the best at what you do, so no hanging about get cracking" With that the men got up and started to leave the office each chomping at the bit to take on the new earn, they knew they would get a slice of the action, pay your workers well and they would remain loyal as he mum said and she was right, he had the best crew and business was thriving. "Jimmy can you hold back I want to have a quick word with you mate" Jimmy nodded and went to the bar, Linda had laid on some bagels for the boys as she called them, Jimmy loved a bit of salmon and cream cheese, as the room cleared Jimmy sat down and Adam and Stevie joined him" Listen Jim it's not the usual favour, I need you to plot one of the younger boys up outside Nancy's for a couple of weeks just to keep an eye out I have seen Billy's handywork and his a bitter spiteful little fucker I don't think he will be to happy when he realises I'm seeing Nancy" Jimmy nodded while eating his bagel "no worries I have a younger in mind that won't mind earning a few quid" "actually Jim while your round there pop in and see Sue her son is called Tyrone, his a proper lump and is a heavy in the making you might want to meet him and his mum and take him under your wing, I'm hearing good things about him, his only 14 the youngers are the future let's get him in with us now, his well-liked on the manor and is already earning a reputation for looking after his own and I like that" Jimmy's eyes gleamed in agreement, you will always find a heavy but every now and again there's was one that shone out and come up in the ranks quick he would go and meet old Sue and the boy and suss the situation out, "consider it done mate, everything will be in place by the end of the day"

As Jimmy left Linda came in and gave Adam a wad of messages, she looked at him one eyebrow raised "there's a couple in there from the wife she sounds a bit pissed off boy you missed her weekly call, you better get on the blower to her" Adam smiled up at Linda "I will give her a bell in a minute, do you need me to sign any cheques or anything?" Linda laughed "Adam I have been signing your cheques for ten years or didn't you notice?" Adam laughed, she's a case our Linda "and while you're here call the accountant his a pain in the arse" Stevie laughed no one spoke to them like that only Linda, she really was a law onto herself, she was the backbone of the firm, she knew the deals on or off the books and never breathed a word, at fifty years of age she kept a brick in her handbag by the side of the desk and a shooter in the office and she wasn't afraid to use either. As she left the room Stevie faced Adam "so lover boy how are you, I can't believe you disappeared your looking good", which was the truth Adam looked happy, like he had his spark back. Adam smiled a genuine smile " I'm happy, I think I have met someone that I have finally connected with I can feel it, I never felt this with Debbie never, and I don't know where its taking me but I'm going to enjoy it" Adam spoke from the heart there was no lying in him as he looked at Stevie " I want what you and Patsy have, I have never had that ever and I feel like I have a chance at it with Nancy life's too short bruv, what's the point of all this as he looked around the boardroom "if we have got no one to share it with" Steve nodded in agreement "too true little brother too true"

Back East Nancy was sitting at the table lost deep in the memories of the last few days, the smoke from the cigarette was rising through the air in swirls from her fingers, her glass of vodka was untouched the ice had melted and the condensation had left a pool of water around the glass, the ash was dropping onto the table but Nancy was oblivious, she felt like she had been struck by lightning, in all the years she had been on the streets no one had ever got under her skin like Adam Donnelly. Nancy had connected with him like she had no other, even the smell of him intoxicated her, they were in tune, and for the first time in her life she felt safe, Billy was now a distant memory, she would tell him to his face it was over if she had too, she didn't know where this was leading but she knew that while she was with this hunk of a man that filled her every thought she was done with the game. She was roused from her stupor when she heard a loud bang and Ronnie came rushing through to the kitchen all flushed cheeks and skinny legs, Ronnie dropped her bag and threw her arms around her mum, "hello mum you ok" Nancy looked at her as if she was really seeing her for the first time, this slip of a girl that was passed from pillar to post and was neglected for days on end never judged her, loved her unconditionally, Nancy knew that the bond was broken with the girl and vowed to try and work to make things better she smiled back at little Ronnie "did you enjoy staying down with Aunty Sue she told me you was a good girl and you helped her out with little Terry you have such a good heart I don't know where you get it from" Ronnie preened at the compliments her mum had given, unused to it she smiled shyly " thanks mum it was lovely Aunty Sue made macaroni cheese and this stuff called curry goat! I don't think it was a goat it tasted like beef it was a curry mum spicy with rice I loved it" Nancy smiled at Ronnie "I'm glad you liked it listen how about we go get some fish and chips tonight I'm not working and we stay home and watch some telly you know I love the equaliser Edward Woodwood is my favourite" Ronnie's mouth dropped in shock "really mum we can watch some telly and the new equaliser" Ronnie was shaking with excitement, dinner and my mum at home! It doesn't get better than this wow and she is in a good mood! As they walked down to the shops Nancy and Ronnie was oblivious to the man watching them discreetly from afar he followed them to the chip shop and back while they nattered on Nancy holding their bag of chips and Ronnie with her big bottle of Tizer, as they went back into the flats Shainey reported in to Jimmy that was sitting up Sues table, he whispered in his ear and Jimmy nodded acknowledgement and Shainey slipped back out of the house and sat back in his ford RS 2000 a serious bit of motor that could drive like the wind when needed it was his pride and joy.

"So Sue Adam has told me that your Tyrone is earning a good name, I know Roger is already working his own thing but I have made a few enquires myself and looking at him I can see what they mean about him, Sue looked at her boy with pride, "his a good boy Mr Donnelly" "please call me Jimmy" he smiled across at her while sizing up the boy "fuck me what you been feeding him women his the size of a brick shit house" the table erupted in laughter, "listen boy I want you to come down to the boxing club, you can help out we will send your ma home a bit of poke, you will earn a little wedge and we will take you under our wing and show you the ropes I have a feeling in my water that you are going to be a bit of a handful, your reputation is already proceeding you I heard you took care a couple of boys the other day with a baseball bat" he looked across at Tyrone appraising the size of him "you will be a great asset to my team what do you say boy" Tyrone looked at him thoughtfully and smiled "sounds like a plan Mr Donnelly" "please call me Jimmy" he smiled magnanimously "you're part of the firm now boy" Jimmy shook the boys hand and stood up from the table "I've left one of my boys outside Sue he will be keeping an eye on Nancy for the next couple of weeks if you see Billy lurking about this is my number or just tell the boy outside for me babe" he slipped a little business card gave her a kiss on the cheek "I must be off now the missus made me a roast and if I'm late I will be wearing the dinner not eating it" Sue laughed these Donnelly's were a right bunch but she liked them! Jimmy jumped in the car and sped home, as soon as he got in he rang Adam updated him assuring him that everything was in place around Nancy, Adam thanked him and hung the phone up. Adam then dialled Debbie it rang a few times before she picked up "hello Deb you've left a couple of messages for me is everything ok?" "of course it is I just wondered if he was going to with your grace me with your presence this week" she replied flatly "I will be home for dinner on Sunday" he always went home on a Sunday no matter what and ate dinner, the marriage was dead he knew that now more than ever "do you need anything" he asked "What I want you can't give me" in his head he thought here we go again, he choked back his resentment and replied nicely" I have to go I have got a bit of business to deal with I'll see you on Sunday ok" he realised the silence was not a reply she had already put the phone down, she was a right moody fucker, he shook his head and poured himself another scotch now let's deal with that little squirt Billy.

Billy was making his way down to Soho thoroughly pissed off, not only had Nancy disappeared he was also being summoned like some little errand boy to the Donnelly's offices the earlier buzz of being involved with them was already wearing thin he felt a shift in the work force nothing had been said but he could see the way the crew were looking at him, it lacked the respect that as far as he was concerned he commanded, he couldn't put his finger on it but he knew something was brewing. Nancy was definitely going to get a right hander when he laid his eyes on her she had took the piss out of him royally he had heard a whisper on the street that she was shacked up with someone, no names were mentioned, well he would find out who it was and cut the pair of them together that would put the crew back in order, he smirked at the thought now let's go see what these mugs want.

As Billy drove along he had already had his master plan well thought out, within a few years he would wipe out the whole clan of fucking Donnelly's and own the pavement he was so sure of it, he walked into the club like he owned it, looking at the smiles of the doorman and staff not realising they were looking at him and thinking what a complete mug he was. As he made his way up to the offices he was shocked to walk into a modern light office that took over the whole of the second floor, he stood at the window and watched the passing crowds of people all going about their everyday lives, from office workers to tourists he raised his nose in contempt their all easy marks the lots of them, they were beneath him as far as he was concerned. He turned when he heard the office door open and watched as Adam and Stevie walked in, Adam walked across the room and Stevie's sheer size filled the doorframe he was again reminded that these men were a proper handful and cleared his throat "alright fellas" Adam smiled and shook his hand "let's take a seat" and pointed to a chair opposite the modern glass desk, as Adam sat down at the desk Stevie sat down on the deep leather coach that was behind Billy, "no problems getting down here Bill?" Adam enquired politely Billy shook his head "Steve do me a favour fix me and Billy a nice drink" "no problem" this was Adams show and he wanted to sit back and have a ring side seat for this one, this little pricks come up pence has been a long time coming he mused as he poured out a liberal measure of scotch, his going to need this drink when he realises what's coming, Stevie sauntered over and handed the drinks over to both men and then poured himself a cup of tea, he was a tea man all day long when I die they best put a box of PG Tips in with me, he had given his Patsy instructions to that effect, did she laugh at that one!

As Stevie sat down, Adam begun, "right Billy there's a few things I want to sort out, firstly Nancy" Billy's head snapped up in shock "Nancy?" Adam nodded his head "yes Nancy, from today she no longer exists to you don't contact her, trouble her, look at her, if you go near her or her kid we will have a very big problem with each other, do you understand Billy" Billy clocked on straight away ah so this was the mysterious fella, he silently applauded her, well done Nancy you have landed yourself a big fish. Billy smirked knowing exactly how to rile Adam up he went in for the jugular " what's the interest in that old brass? she has had more dirty cocks then a dockers dolly mate she" before he could finish his sentence Adam jumped up and pounced across the desk that divided them, Adam roared like a bear as he grabbed Billy by the throat and threw him against the wall as Billy landed Adam was already there, for his size he moved fast, he was nose to nose with Billy as he snarled "now I knew that with a mug like you this was not going to easy, you're out, your crew is now my crew, I have taken over the northern connections, I'm taking your houses and share of your clubs, on the table is a cheque take it cash it and fuck off, it's a fair price and I would prefer you vanished, no one wants or likes you on this manor you're finished" that cheque is your only offer" Billy looked at Adam, and without a word, walked over and picked up the cheque and put it in his top pocket, he walked from the room without a backwards glance, he knew at that moment he was bested by the brothers, but every dog has its day mate and I will have mine, he repeated it to himself over and over until he got back to one of the houses in Ilford. The anger was raging through his body, as Billy walked in one of his boys was already there waiting "Terry...." Terry held up his hand and stopped hm "listen Bill I work for Mr Donnelly now and you're going to have to leave your no longer allowed on any of the premises Mr Donnelly has left me strict instructions you're going to have to go" Billy was raging but looking at the sheer size of Terry he retreated, knowing while Terry wasn't the sharpest knife in the drawer one punch off that meaty fist was enough to knock a few teeth out, and put you out cold, underneath it all Billy was a bully but a coward, he turn around and stormed off. As he drove back to his flat it took every shred of self-control that he had left in him not to wrap himself around a lamp post. Billy was shaking so much it took five attempts to put the key in the lock, he slammed the door on his flat shut and went to the bedroom where he pulled the safe open grabbing the large wads of money, he then checked his bank accounts moody and straight and thought fuck this I'm out of here, he hastily threw clothes into a suitcase and pulled out his passport, reaching for his the phone he booked the next flight to Marbella he already had a plan forming in his head he had mates over there, he would get back on his feet and plot his revenge this day would never be forgotten............

Chapter four

Everything fell into place quickly, all of the transition was smooth, the girls were a lot happier the northern connection was as lucrative as Adam had envisioned and the bars were turning over nice, on the whole it was a good result, as Adam drove back through Loughton he followed the country lanes through till he got to his destination, he pressed the button on his remote and the electric gates opened on his home in Chigwell the drive cut through immaculate landscaped grounds, the house itself was set in a few acres of land and had tennis courts, stables and a beautiful swimming pool that sat next to a sprawling property. The leaded windows sparkled in the sunlight, this house needed a family it needed arms and legs everywhere the children's park that sat by the tennis court had never been used, the swings had never been sat on they just moved aimlessly when the breeze took them. Debbie have never invited any of the family to the house not even for a sausage on a BBQ, Adam wondered if he had allowed her to get away with too much, after the second miscarriage Debbie was prescribed medication to battle the depression, she promptly attempted an overdose, in the end she became so unhinged she had to be committed, Mrs swan the housekeeper found her running around the grounds naked with a can of petrol and a lighter, the tennis court had gone up like a roman candle. The doctors levelled her out on a combination of medication and therapy, she now attended an outpatient programme in a lovely private facility.   The person he had fell in love with disappeared, she came out of the hospital broken, all that was left was a shell, they carried on trying for a baby but nothing happened, they tried doctors, specialists but in the end Adam lost heart.

Debbie slowly pushed him away and he started to feel like a guest in his own home, Debbie had insisted on separate bedrooms, the house became cold and sterile it was so unwelcoming his friends made excuses to not come over for dinner so in the end he stopped inviting them, he knew it was because Debbie made them feel uncomfortable fuck she made him feel the same way, in the end he started staying away, spending more and more time at the flat to the point he only returned on Sundays for dinner, he made sure she wanted for nothing not that she ever left the house, he was exhausted from trying, he eventually asked for a divorce but Debbie refused flatly stating she was a catholic and it was a sin, he didn't have the heart to push it so they fell into the routine of one phone call and a dinner a week. Meeting Nancy blew all of this to pieces he knew that she was a completely different entity, when they were lying in bed together, they cuddled! He smiled at the thought of her, the companionship that he craved was finally given to him, they lay there all night talking about their pasts, nothing was left out the good or bad, Nancy legs was entwinned with his, as she padded out to the kitchen in his shirt and nothing else and come back with two cups of tea and lit him a cigarette he was sold, he didn't want her to leave, in fact he was going to her tonight to surprise her, he needed her that alone was a revelation in itself.

As he turned off the engine and walked into the house he looked around it was as usual perfection, a show home, the cushions on the sofa all standing proudly to attention the rooms were beautifully decorated all cream and gold very understated and not over powering it truly was a beautiful home, he heard a noise and looked up, Debbie paused at the top of the staircase to make sure he was ready for her grand entrance and made her way down the stairs slowly, she was groomed to perfection not a hair out of place, her face was expertly made up but none the less a mask, she used to have a lovely figure, curvy now she was painfully thin, her hair was burnished gold, the subtle streaks were gleaming in the late afternoon sun "hello Adam we have lamb today followed by a fruit crumble that Mrs Swan has made" "that will be lovely, I do like Mrs Swans crumbles" he cleared his throat "any chance of a cuppa? I'm parched" she wrinkled her nose at what she considered common street slang and nodded as she walked into the kitchen, he sat himself up the marble counter top that also doubled as a breakfast bar and watched her closely as she put the kettle on " that smells lovely Deb " she didn't reply just methodically put the teabag and sugar in the cup and walked over to the fridge to get the milk out " how have you been?" she just smiled and past him the cup "I'm ok Adam never better" he could see how this was going to play out already it was like watching paint dry, "the garden looks lovely" "yes the gardener has been in this week and cut the grass and planted the beds as you drive in" "are you ready for Mrs Swan to serve the dinner now?" he nodded and followed her into the dining room the table was set and shining to perfection.

Dinner was painful the silence stretched between them for what felt like an eternity, after eating his desert, he cleared his throat and looked at her, she really was a good looking women, "I'm done Debbie as always it was lovely" she patted the sides of her mouth gently with her napkin " you best be off leave the plates there I will clear it all" "are you sure?" " yes go on you be off now I know your busy" he looked at her for a minute and could see the deadpan expression on her face and shrugged she was actually starting to make his skin crawl "ok then I will set off now and with give you a call in the week ok" she smiled up at him and rose from her chair, she walked to the door and opened it, Adam stopped and went to kiss her cheek but as he moved forward she flinched and stepped back, he straightened his shoulders "bye Deb till next week" Adam walked away trying to shake off the sadness that hung around hm like a cloak of doom, Debbie watched him climb into his car, just closing the door, and slowly walking back into the dining room.

As Adam drove out of the gates, he breathed a sigh of relief, it was not getting any easier, Debbie was a burden, it was getting more difficult to keep the charade going, he didn't know how to deal with it anymore he knew sooner or later the situation would reach a breaking point, but right now he was honestly at a loss.

As he drove back through Loughton, he's mind strayed back to Nancy and before he knew it as if on autopilot he was turning off the motorway and driving through Bow, sod it I'm going to pop round for a cup of tea as he drove through Bethnal Green stopping off, he bought a big bouquet of flowers and then running into the off licence next door he picked up a couple of bottles of wine and some sweets and fizzy pop for little Ronnie he was grinning from ear to ear like a naughty little schoolboy. He jumped back in the car and drove the short distance to Tomlinson close. As he pulled up he spotted Jimmy's man plotted up in a car nodding in acknowledgement at the boy Adam had already heard that Billy had fled the country with his tail between his leg, he decided Shaine could stay put a little longer just as a precaution. Adam took the bag and flowers out of the car and walked into the block of flats, climbing the stairs two at a time he made his way to Nancy's flat.

"Ronnie answer the door babe " Nancy shouted down the stairs as she was just brushing her hair after getting out of the bath Ronnie run and open the door thinking it was Sue and was shocked to see a giant of a man she had never see before looking down at her "hello you must be Ronnie?" "who are you" Ronnie asked not in the least bit scared "I'm a friend of your mums my names Adam" Nancy looked over the bannisters from upstairs and couldn't believe Adam was standing on her door step with flowers! she wrapped a robe around herself and run down the stairs grinning from ear to ear "this is a nice surprise what are you doing here" "I thought I'd pop round for a glass of wine and maybe get a takeaway in with you and your girl what do you say?" looking down at little Ronnie winking at her, Ronnie's eyes looked up at him wide like saucers, "well I don't know" Nancy laughed "what do you think?" Looking down at little Ronnie as she nodded her head "well come in then" Nancy laughed taking the huge bouquet of flowers out of Adams hands she blushed "no one's bought me flowers before" he looked into her eyes and smiled "this is just the beginning".

The evening was an eye opener for Adam he popped over to the Bagel shop and bought a Selection of filled bagels, they sat down with plates on their laps Ronnie sat on the floor trying to see how many Maltesers she could wedge into her mouth at once He laughed and joked with them both and literally soaked up everything like a sponge he was completely comfortable and at ease in his surroundings, shoes were kicked off and Nancy was curled up next to him, he had to laugh to himself, he had property's worth and he couldn't settle in any of them and here he was in a tiny council flat, the happiest he had ever been. Nancy's face was flushed with happiness, he pulled her closer to him the warmth of her body was all he needed, she looked up at him, "you ok?" He answered honestly "I have never been better" they stared at each other for what felt like a lifetime "mum can I stay up and watch Dempsey and Makepeace?" what do you think?" Nancy laughed "come on Ronnie its bedtime", Ronnie didn't argue she had a belly full of food and sweets, she jumped up night mum she leaned over and kissed her on the cheek, and impulsively she reached over and hugged Adam, Nancy's jaw dropped Ronnie was a strange little fish she never took to no man ever, she run upstairs without a backwards glance, "wow", she shook her head, "she likes you" "funny enough Nancy I like her she is a good kid" "he turned and looked at her, "do you want another glass of wine?" She went to get up from the sofa, Adam jumped up, "no let me get it", she followed him with her eyes and watched him as he hummed to himself in the kitchen, opening the drawer and pulling out the corkscrew he opened the bottle and poured out two glasses, as he walked back into the front room he caught Nancy staring out him he stopped in his tracks "did I forget something?" Nancy looked at him her eyes glistening with tears "no everything is perfect"

Adam and Nancy spent the night on the sofa taking, it was everything that Adam wished he had in his life, even the silences were comfortable, Nancy yawned and stretched out, "come on" Adam stood up and held out his hand and pulled her up,

Nancy's brow deepened "are you leaving?" "no babe we are going to bed" he kissed her deeply and they walked up to her room, one of the good things about Ronnie was the house was always spotlessly clean, the bedroom smelt of washing powder and lenor fabric conditioner. Adam stripped off and Nancy took off her robe, they slipped into bed as they faced each other, Adam reached over to her and with one scoop pulled her against him, she was as aroused as he was, he kissed her deeply and pulled the silk night slip above her head, he trailed her body with kisses and entered her smooth and deep, as he was thrusting into her, he held himself above her and looked into her eyes bending down he kissed her face and slowly swirled his tongue inside her mouth, biting her lip he smiled as he watched her face with every thrust he could fell the build-up in her body and his, and pushed into her harder and faster loosing himself, she wrapped her legs around his waist and pulled him into her even deeper, she wanted to feel every inch of him, he looked at her and smiled, he bent down and kissed her deeply and let himself go, he climaxed long and hard inside her, he truly now understood what he had been missing in his life this was more than sex this was love. They spent the night whispering and talking about their hopes for the future, kissing each other deeply they become lost to each other over and over again, as the sun came up Adam was still making love to Nancy, she was blown away with the feelings this man had awoke in her, as he kissed her face and nestled behind her, they finally fell asleep as the birds started to sing.

Nancy woke to the smell of bacon and the sound of laughter she could hear the radio on low and Ronnie laughing, which in turn made her giggle to herself, she stretched out and slipped out of the bed, as she looked in the mirror she was glowing, she smiled back at her reflection and quickly brushed her hair, she ran to the bathroom quickly brushing her teeth and walked slowly downstairs. The sight that welcomed her she swore she would never forget as long as she lived the kitchen looked like it had been blown up and standing at her cooker was Adam cooking up a breakfast! She looked over at Ronnie who was buttering thick slices of bread and could not believe eyes, as she watched them they were unaware that she was in the kitchen "so Ronnie, what's your school like?" its ok but my Teacher Mr Coffee is a bit of a pain he don't like me and sometimes he digs me out" "does he know, well don't worry girl we will get that sorted "as he looked down at this little munchkin he caught a glimpse of Nancy " well hello madam is awake! Just in time too, sit down breakfast is served" Nancy did as she was told and sat at the table tea and bread courtesy of Ronnie was promptly put in front of her and as if by magic plates of hot steaming breakfast was put on the table and wonders will never cease it looked edible! "me and little legs were up early so we went and got some breakfast in and we also see Sue, Adam winked at Nancy she has kindly agreed to watch Ronnie tonight were going out for a bit of dinner, how's that sound, Nancy looked at him as he was dipping his bread into his fried egg, she looked over at Ronnie who was nodding her head "go on mum Aunty Sues making me a stew tonight she reckons it going to put meat on my bones!" Nancy laughed picking up her knife and fork "alright then it's a date" the breakfast was demolished with gusto; Adam sat back and watched the little tableau and knew his cup had truly runneth over.

And this was how it begun, nights out and nights in, Nancy noticed the clothing creeping into her wardrobe and drawers, his razors and aftershaves were in her bathroom, she held up a shirt to her nose and took a deep breath inhaling his scent, she folded his shirts with care and placed them in the chest of drawers, then it got to the point Adam never left and she no longer slept alone. Nancy had a purse full of money and a fridge full of food, it was like a weight had been lifted from her shoulders, most nights they were in her flat, but Sue also watched Ronnie so they could also slip off to his flat in Wapping, he laughed "come on your walls are too bloody thin we need to show a degree of decorum" the sex was mind-blowing and a revelation for the both of them, the workforce noticed the change in the boss and they were happy for him his wife was a 24 carat pain in the ass not exactly Mrs popularity with the other wives and as far as they were concerned everyone deserved to be happy, so what if her past was a bit dicey, they weren't going to say a dickie bird as far as that were concerned good luck to him, as Stevie remarked dryly "his like a dog with three fucking lampposts" that was the comment of the day as the boys laughed.

"Nancy were out tonight babe for dinner, and were taking Ronnie as well" Nancy walked in from the kitchen with two mugs of tea, as always looking as sexy as fuck as far as Adam was concerned, "were going to my mums for dinner" laughing as Nancy's face went white with fear "and everyone's going to be there" "you might as well get it over with they have been chewing my ear holes for the past fortnight" Nancy smiled weakly she was terrified and it showed, sod it "ok let's get this show on the road" after trying on three different outfits she decided that Ronnie looked beautiful in her new clothes her hair was pulled up into a high ponytail and fell in natural curls, as they skipped out to the car Nancy followed, Sue as ever was sitting outside with her rum and coke watching them from afar, as Adam opened the door for little Ronnie her heart hurt in her chest when she caught the sweet look that past between them, she knew that Nancy and Adam were topic of conversation on the estate, but to see that little family as she just did she truly wished them all the best, she knew Nancy was a fucker, but it looked to her like she was trying with the girl and that they were all a whole lot happier she waved at them as they drove off, ever nosey she wondered where they were all going, she smiled knowing that little Ronnie would spill the beans tomorrow when she come in to see Terry.

As Adam drove along he placed his hand over Nancy's and smiled at her "you're going to be fine trust me they don't bite" Nancy wasn't so sure her old insecurities were battling against her, as if sensing what she was thinking, he tightened his grip on her hand and reassured her, "Nancy I promise you everything will be ok", Nancy looked into his eyes and smiled "ok let's do this" as they pulled up Nancy looked around "I didn't know your mum lived here", Adam smiled "my mother has lived in spring walk all her life, raised thirteen of us in that house she refuses to leave it, she knows everyone not just on this street but the estate, after our dad passed away she prefers to be surrounded by her family and friends, the first thing we did when we earned money was buy this house for our mum and dad" he opened the doors for the girls to get out "Ronnie run ahead go knock on the red door there sweetheart" pointing ahead of him, Ronnie run along exited and knocked on the door.

As it opened a little petite lady with a mop of curled blond hair smiled at her, "ah you must be Ronnie I'm Puna aren't you a pretty little thing" she put out her arms and Ronnie automatically went to them, she hugged the little girl tightly, Ronnie loved her on sight, she took a deep breath and smelt the lavender and washing powder and sighed it was a smell she would never forget, "go in sweetheart you have got a front room full of people waiting to meet you" Ronnie slipped past and ran down the hallway with not one jot of fear exited to meet Adams family, Adam walked up to his mother holding Nancy's hand, "hello mum this is Nancy" Puna looked at the beautiful girl that stood before her, she smiled she could see why Adam was taken by the girl she was stunning, "blimey you look like a movie start your eyes remind me of Liz Taylor" Nancy laughed and kissed her on the cheek "if only" "come in let's get the kettle on" As Nancy walked through the door the only way to describe what greeted her was bedlam the fear fell away the moment she walked over the doorstep, the house was beautiful, the boys had obviously had major renovations done throughout. She walked through the downstairs of the house the kitchen and living room were open plan and had been extended into the garden, there was two massive tables set up and two small ones, all the grandchildren were already seated, Ronnie was already in the middle of the table, centre of attention all the kids were curious, uncle Adam had never brought anyone to dinner, ever! As they walked through the conversations all came to an abrupt halt, Puna waved to the two chairs empty near the top of the table and Adam grabbed Nancy's hand to sit down, she had her sisters in to help prepare the dinner they had been baking up a storm all day, delicious aromas were escaping the kitchen and everyone including Ronnie was drooling waiting for the dinner to be served, the plates were quickly brought from the kitchen piping hot as everyone got stuck in , Nancy watched everyone at the table and smiled if only she had this as a child she would have stood half a chance, she knew she had a sister out there somewhere but when they were taken into care, they had been separated, Nancy was a few years older and had promptly run away from every home they placed her in.

 Puna smiled at Nancy breaking her thoughts "so my Adam has told me so much about you, tell me a little about yourself" Nancy put down her knife and fork and finished chewing her dinner, "there's not much to say really, my mum died when I was young in child birth we were originally from Ireland, but my dad moved us over here for work, he couldn't cope though, he could just about look after himself let alone me and my little sister, we eventually ended up in care, she was adopted out straight away bit I went from foster homes to children homes, as soon as I was 16 I run away and made my way to London" she closed her eyes remembering the things that she couldn't say out loud, what her father did to her it was her secret and it was safely looked away in her heart hidden so it could not hurt her anymore. Puna looked into Nancy's eyes and see the hurt there, one thing about the women in this family they had the intuition to see into a person's soul and see the things that were left unsaid, Puna didn't probe any further she didn't have too, she placed her hand over Nancy's and squeezed it gently "you have a lovely little girl there, to be sure when she grows up she will be a looker like you" she looked at her son who was lit up like a Christmas tree "do you love my boy" Nancy looked into her eyes, and she welled up "yes, yes I do" Puna patted her hand and picked up her knife and fork and started to eat she looked up and winked at her son, she liked her.

The night was a success, Ronnie was having a ball and Nancy for the first time in her life felt comfortable in her own skin and surroundings they welcomed her with open arms, all curious but not to nosey, Adam had never brought one of his girls home before so they knew this was serious, Adam and Nancy moved as one and everyone could see they were smitten with each other. As they waved good bye and kissed Puna on the cheek, Nancy went and sat in the car and she was literally grinning like a Cheshire cat, the relief that swept through her body was overwhelming they hadn't even got to the end of the road and Ronnie was already asleep on the back seat she had the time of her life a belly full of food and was now out cold, Nancy looked across at her Adam who was humming to a song on the radio and wanted to kiss him so she leaned over and did, life was finally feeling good.

Puna walked back into the house and sat with her girls and sisters, everything was already back to sparkling and with the clearing down out of the way the serious business was now at hand, tea was poured, fags were lit and they all sat down together, "well girls all I can say is I like her" Susie scoffed "she is a brass mum" "so what" Puna replied "do you know how many mothers had to moonlight and sell their ass's to put food on the tables for their kids to survive? too many!" she looked around the table and made sure she had their full attention, "that girl has pulled herself up through shit that we have never had to endure to survive and I'm telling you this my boy is in love with her and she loves him" wiping a tear from her cheek she looked across the table "he has been married to that bitter bitch for 20 years when have you ever seen her at our table? when was the last time we sat at hers? have any of you have seen my Adam look how he does right now? Forget about her past she is now one of us" "and if anyone out there" pointing at the door "says overwise you will all have her back understood?" they nodded their heads in agreement, Puna raise her hand and clenched her fist "the thing with us is the power is in our numbers that girl has never had family, and while she is with our boy she has us, agreed" they all nodded in agreement.

Chapter five

"Look Nancy I don't want you going back to the life" Nancy sighed "Adam I have got to work I am going out of my mind with boredom during the day I have to have something for myself to keep me occupied, I'm going stir crazy" Adam laughed "listen how about I put you in one of the clubs and you run the girls, and make sure no one is ripping off the take I have a lovely little bar in Soho that needs sorting out what do you say?" Nancy blew her cigarette smoke out and smiled at him gently "what would I do without you" he reached across to her hand "no babe what would I do without you".

Life had fell into a comfortable routine, days were spent at work and evenings they were together, they even had cheeky little weekends away, Adam adored Ronnie she was a little firecracker, he proudly told anybody that listened, Ronnie suddenly found herself surrounded by multiple cousins, they all accepted her like she was one of their own and she began to flourish, her life now had a routine, she had a good home life, good food and an abundance of love from a large family, Nancy still struggled from time to time but their relationship had finally turned a corner.

Adam was driving through the West End "you are going to love this little club Nancy, it's a good earner but needs someone in control we have just took it over, the girls are ok but they need a firm hand you know the drill get the punters in keep them happy, make sure the girls don't fight, and that their clean, no std's or heavy drug use" she nodded in agreement "when we go home tonight I want to talk to you about the flat" Nancy shook her head "I'm not moving Adam I'm happy there Sue is only downstairs I know everybody there and Ron is content I'm not going to rip her away from what she knows and put it in the house in the middle of nowhere" he shook his head in exasperation "I want to give you better" Nancy held her hand up and cut him off "I know you do sweetheart but you've already done enough I'm happy" "Nancy the place needs gutting look, what if we reach a happy solution, in a couple of weeks we go to Tenerife to one of the villas and I'll get the boys in and they can give the place a makeover? they can put in a new kitchen and bathroom and replace everything" Nancy looked indignant "what's wrong with the old furniture?" he laughed "you have money, you can upgrade, it's about having a fresh start babe, now let's start as we mean to go on" Nancy relented and nodded in agreement, she didn't know what to say it was still all so overwhelming for her she was still resisting the bigger gifts! "I don't need you to keep on buying me things, I don't want you to think that I'm with you just for money" he laughed "don't be so stupid if you're going to make me stay in that flat at least let me do it up okay just think about it that's all I'm asking"

As Nancy and Adam drove through the back of Chinatown she looked at all of the bright lanterns swinging from the lamp posts, the vibrant reds and golds looked so pretty against the dull sky, the streets of London never bored her, she loved the hustle and bustle of the West end and how the club was nestled in the back streets of Soho alongside lovely Italian restaurants where they often spent their evenings, she didn't even realise that Adam had owned a club here until he started the conversation about her taking over the day to day management, as he pulled up outside, he jumped out of the driver seat and proceeded to open the door for Nancy, he nodded at big Dave who nodded back he looked back at Nancy "this is my brother from another mother Dave" Nancy looked up at Dave and smiled, thinking I have never seen such a lump in all my life he filled the door he was at least 6 foot 4 "well I'm sure we don't have much trouble in here with you on the door" he chuckled "you would be surprised darling put a couple of brandy's in them and they will all think they are Rocky" Nancy laughed and placed her hand in his "it's a pleasure to meet you" As she walked in she walked down a narrow set of mirrored steps and into a large low lit bar area, it was clad in deep rich dark burgundies, crushed velvets, smoked mirrors, and had heavy sparkling chandeliers hanging from the ceilings Adam waved around the expanse of the bar "there's a large stage area for the dancers lots of private booths around the edging" the tables with were set with candles in a red cut glass holders the low light set the mood. The club smelt of perfume, old whiskey and sex, Nancy knew the smells all too well, she was in her element, comforted by the fact that she would no longer have to turn a trick to earn a pound note she judged the room differently, your here to get these girls under control, at the back there you have some private rooms for the laps dances, behind the bar you have a couple of girls that serve up coke as well as spirits its members only in here so the trouble is kept to a minimum, Nancy looked at him "do you only have the women working the pole in here?" "Why what are you thinking" he could see the light in her eyes as her brain started to work overtime she was like a bloodhound sniffing out a new scent, "I think you should split the bar into alternate nights there is a huge gay community down here, we should have male dancers on that pole and drag acts and women working the following nights ,maybe give the Friday up for the gay night and Saturday for the usual gentlemen club?" Adam nodded in agreement, "that's why I pulled you in for this bar it needs shaking up, Nancy was now on a roll Adam smiled "I'm thinking start with one night a week the Friday like you said and see of it takes off and if it does we will change it up a bit and introduce it slowly so we pull in the new punters and don't lose the old", she nodded in agreement, Adam glanced at his watch and realised he was running late "right listen I'm going to pop to the offices, I'm not far away if you need me, you have a good look around and introduce yourself to everyone and see what you think and then we will sort out a day for you to start" Nancy nodded her mind was already working racing "I'm going to have to do a couple of evenings I think I should definitely be here for the gay night until it gets off the ground", he laughed yep she was already making her mark, he put his hand under her chin and tilted her face up and gently kissed her lips the girls that were all sitting at the bar were already watching them with curiosity, all sighed why couldn't they have that, Nancy had landed right on her feet with Adam what a catch, looking at them staring into each other's eyes made them hope that one day that could happen to them, Adam caught them staring and they all quickly made themselves scarce, he kissed her again "I will be back in a couple of hours ok".

By the time Adam returned, Nancy had fired two of the dancers, she took one look at them and could literally smell the brown coming through their pores, one of them had eyes so dilated she couldn't even stand still, they were a total liability she outed them without a second thought. She got the bar manager to call the cleaners in and gave them a bollocking of epic proportions the place was absolute filth, she told them they had 48 hours to get the place deep cleaned or she would be replacing them with new people, the kitchen was good but she noticed that the chef was ordering stock for his own personal use, did he get the shock of his life when she told him she would be giving Linda all the receipts and order books for the past year and he would be billed accordingly, he untied his apron and ripped of his hat and walked out, the cheek of it he didn't even say good bye! Adam was laughing as big Dave was filling him in, he called one of the managers from the casinos and got a chef sent over to cover the next few nights until they replaced the old one, as he walked in the bar he had to laugh the bar already looked cleaner, everyone was on alert, the bar was sparkling the glasses and optics of spirits was gleaming, oh yes my girl has made her mark. He looked over and see his Nancy sitting in a booth with a cup of tea pouring over the books, "what are you doing we do have Colin the manager, that's his job" "well I've been her nearly five hours and can tell you by what I have seen he is about as much use as a chocolate teapot, so what's it to be are you sacking him or am I?" Adam looked at her like she had grown two heads, he grabbed her face and kissed her hard, he knew there and then that he had finally met the mate he should have had twenty years ago, "why don't we both do it" she patted the seat beside her, he slid in coping a quick feel and she laughed he was too saucy! "I know I have got carried away but I want to prove to you I can do this and I want to repay you for all you have done for me and Ronnie I'm not comfortable just taking money, I want to earn it" he took her cup and took a quick mouthful of tea and turned and kissed her, looking into her eyes he welled up "I would give you the world you know" "well to be honest right now I would settle for a steak and leg over" he roared with laughter, a girl after his own heart! "That's a deal, "come on then let's sort this out and we will go and get you a steak" she gave him a cheeky wink and they got down to business.

That night set the tone for Adams and Nancy working relationship, the gay night was a runaway success, the place was full, the drag acts were the best that she had ever seen of course her all-time favourite was Cher, she had better make up on then Nancy! The girls loved Nancy, the working environment was a lot better, the club was a lot cleaner and it showed, she also found out the bar manager had been having a skim on the spirits so he once he was outed and the take trebled, everyone was happy. Adam was proud of Nancy he had threw her in the deep end and not only did she succeed she had pulled in a whole new list of members, even he was surprised by the names that were in the book, this was another avenue on getting the edge on his protection, the bar was one hundred percent discreet but Adam made a point of keeping information that was worthy, filled away safely for future use, he called it his get out of jail free card.

Adam now included Nancy in most of the legitimate business dealings, he trusted her wholeheartedly and she thrived under the pressure, she was an asset by his side, her clothes were now becoming expensive and the look was understated, as far as Adam was concerned that made her look even sexier, their sex life was electric and he was as obsessed with her as he was the day he met her. It had already been eight months since they had spent their first night together and he had a little surprise for her tonight he didn't know how she would take it, but he had finally got the paperwork back, it was amazing what a few back handers would do he smiled as he felt the envelope in his jacket pocket, she would probably do her nut. He smiled to himself the last time she had gone mad was when they had come back from Tenerife the only thing that had remained the same in the flat was her door key, he chuckled at the memory the boys had total ripped the place out and his mum ever the decorator had done an outstanding job on the place, it took a few days for Nancy to come back down to earth but even she had to admit she loved it the kitchen was the best Magnet had to offer and the bedrooms, oh how she loved her bedroom, even little Ronnie's, it was like a princesses paradise! And the bathroom she had never in her life seen anything like it! And then to top it off, Adam had ripped out Sues kitchen as well and bought her a new leather three piece to say thank you for all the times she had looked after Ronnie when they were working as far as Sue was concerned he could do no wrong the sun shone out of his ass Nancy often remarked when Sue was singing his praises, Nancy had sarcastically remarked one day let me check your feet because that women thinks you walk on fucking water, he wet himself laughing, in the end she was laughing with him.

He suddenly sobered up with the thought of Debbie he still went to her on a Sunday but not every week, she didn't seem to care he had begged her for a divorce but she still point blank refused to entertain the idea, he knew he was running out of options and would have to get the matter resolved she could have the house and a settlement he would always make sure she was alright but he now see it for what it was, he had his little family now, he hadn't told her about Nancy but surely she must of known. Adam was like a new man, when he visited Debbie now it was like entering a time warp he moved a picture frame one day as a joke, when he went back into the room she had already put it back in its place, shaking with anger as she polished it over and over again, the house was easily worth over a million pounds, but you know what he was happier in that little council flat in Bethnal Green, that was where he took his shoes off every night, that was now his home, Nancy said the bonus of Adam living there was no one pissed in the lift anymore what a cheeky mare, the laughter was never ending and he was the happiest he had ever been.

As he pushed the thought of Debbie out of his mind he smiled when he see Nancy walk out of the club door waving good bye to Dave she looked for Adams car and smiled as she rushed towards it, he opened the door from the inside and pushed the door open, she slid into the passenger seat and reached across to give him a kiss "hello my baby how was your day? let's go straight home I have a surprise for Ronnie one of the drag artists had made Ronnie a little puffball skirt with sequins on it" she knew Ronnie would love it! As they made their way back through the busy streets of West London, Nancy noticed that Adam was nervous "come on then spit it out what's happened" there was no secrets between them "nothing babe what makes you think that?" "you have that look about you Donnelly I know you inside out fella come on spill the beans" he had to smile at her she truly had a nose better than a blood hound he couldn't keep anything from her "listen when we get back to the flat I want to have a little chat ok nothing bad before you give me the Spanish inquisition, I just want to have a little chat" Nancy didn't like it one bit, she was always scared that something would happen to them, it was now her only fear, she looked at him worried "are you sure everything is ok?" "of course it is you lemon come on let's get home and have a cuppa, I'm sure Ronnie will be going to bed with that skirt on tonight" eying up the emerald green tulle and hot pink sequins she laughed yes that was Ronnie summed up if she loved an outfit you literally had to peel it off her body!

As Nancy and Adam walked in Ronnie was not far behind them, Sue had sent her up in her nightie and she burst in excitedly, her eyes looking at the sequins that were shining sitting on the side in the kitchen, Nancy laughed as she run towards them, "yes it was made for you now give me a cuddle and up to bed young lady" Ronnie didn't need telling twice she hugged Adam with her hand full of sparkle running upstairs exited to try on the latest creation! Nancy kicked her shoes off and padded over to the kettle, she run her hand across the smooth cold worktop and marvelled at the shining appliances, she still had to pinch herself, on impulse she turned on the spot to see Adam standing leaning against the doorframe, she walked up to him and put both of her hands on his face and gently kissed his mouth "whatever happens in our life I want you to know I will never love anyone or thing like I love you, you Mr Donnelly are the love of my life" he smiled as her lips touched his, feeling the pull of her, he got lost in her mouth and put his arms around her waist pulling her closer, she pulled her face back and looked into his eyes, "Adam I can't wait no longer, what's wrong, what do you need to tell me, it's nothing bad baby I promise, I just want you to know that everything I do is to make you secure" he pushed her away gently "make us a cuppa let's sit down and we will have a little chat" Nancy made the teas and walked into her newly decorated front room, gone was the fireplace, and in its place was cream thick carpet and a beautiful soft leather sofa, the fireplace had been replaced with a marble one which had a large gold mirror hanging above it, it was all very subtle even the lamps coordinated with the new heavy curtains that now graced her windows she sat down heavily and put her cup on the little table by the side of the sofa and faced Adam. He cleared his throat and reached into his inside pocket and pulled out a thick fold of paperwork, "listen I can't get you out of this flat, and I will be dammed if I'm having my girl in a council place, so I had Linda pull in a few favours and we had your right to buy put through, we have bought the flat it's all paid for and in your name, so you have this as security, you will never lose this home" Nancy just sat on the sofa frozen, he placed all the paperwork in her hands, "it's all been done legit, we greased a few palms to get this done quickly, but I want you to understand this, I love you and little Ronnie, you are my life, but in the end, I want to have a home with a garden and I want you to have better, I want you to have my name, I am working on that now, I cannot be without you" she put her hands up to his mouth to stop him talking and slid across the sofa and wrapped her arms around his neck, "thank you thank you" she whispered in his ear as tears rolled down her face, "so you're not pissed off with me then" he knew how fiercely independent Nancy was she laughed "no I'm not because for the first time in my life I want all them things too, I want to be your wife, I don't care how long as it takes I want you" the feeling of safety that come from having her home given to her was one she would be eternally grateful for, she had deeds! It blew her mind, everything was moving so fast, that was one thing she would always say about her Adam he was a man of his word.

Chapter Six

Mary was walking through to Hatton gardens, she pulled her coat around her, and pulled the belt tight she was feeling the cold today, as she waited to cross the road she fumed as she thought of another day in the office, the jewellers and safety deposit box company had recently been sold and she had gone over to the new owners, it had started good, but as the old staff were rowed out and replaced by family or fresh faces she knew that once they had wrung every last drop from her she would be given her marching orders, she had been with Sonny Rubin for what felt like a life time. Mary had started in the offices, and had gradually took a gemmology course as well as set up the safety deposits boxes, she loved diamonds she had ate slept and breathed the business, and then Sonny decided to retire, his children didn't want the business so he had sold it on, he was crafty really because she didn't get a penny not even a thanks or a farewell drink she thought bitterly, lying in bed last night she couldn't sleep she was that angry, she knew that she would end up walking away with pittance to show for the work she had put in, it kept her awake all night but as the sun come up she had the first spark of an plan, now she had set a meeting up with her mums oldest friend Puna, if anyone would be able to make this happen it would be the Donnelly's. The thought of what she was going to walk away with brought a delicious smile to her face, as her new favourite actor said I love it when a plan comes together, oh how she loved the A team!

Across London Adam was sitting behind his desk, he was bored, he wanted the next earn, he always had a few irons in the fire, and it was time for him to hunt down the next job to keep his juices flowing, his mind wandered and he smiled at the memory of last night, his Nancy was very happy and made sure that when he left to go to work today he had felt the her full appreciation, bloody hell she was a handful alright. He picked up the phone and rung Debbie now more than ever he wanted some kind of finality to that chapter in his life, after a few rings Mrs swan picked up the phone, "hello my lovely how is she" Adam enquired, Mrs swan kept it simple, "Debbie was being her usual self, a right pain in the ass, they didn't speak from one day to the next, her pills were like a cosh to the point she just drifted through her days" "I'm going to come to dinner tonight, I know it's not a Sunday but I have to speak to her and get some things sorted out" Mrs swans heart sunk she was not surprised and knew it was brewing, she could see the change in him and was shocked it had taken Adam this long to finally throw in the towel. Mrs Swan had heard a few whispers, and didn't really blame him he had tried everything to make the women happy, "I'll have a stew going for tonight boy and will set the table for two, but I don't think she will be too happy" Adam snorted "fuck her it's my house I will be over at seven" he hung the phone up and fumed having to ask permission to go to his own home was a joke, he realised now that he was no longer bothered, after tonight Debbie would be in no doubt it was over and he get that divorce.

As Mrs swan hung up Debbie glided into the kitchen, "was that Mr Donnelly?" "Yes Mrs, he is coming home to see you tonight and is stopping for some dinner" "Dinner? Does he not realise it's a weekday he doesn't come to the house during the week?" "Well it is his home; does he need permission to come and see you?" Debbie looked at Mrs Swan as if she had grown another head, after a few minutes she just turned and walked upstairs and slowly walked in to her bedroom, her sanctuary, as she closed the door she put her fist in her mouth to stop herself from screaming, the thought of Adam coming to the house was enough to make her shake from head to toe, the love she had felt for him was long gone and in its place was a slow burning hatred that she had nurtured from the resentment and bitterness of him not being able to give her a child. She had pushed all the conversations she had with the doctor, it was not her it was him, the doctor had told her, the womb was so damaged from the last miscarriage she would never be able to conceive and safely have another child, she had placed that last nugget from the doctor in a little box and filled it away in the deep recesses of her mind, she had never told Adam that, he didn't deserve to know, she hated him and his family, they were all loud brash people that as far as she was concerned were beneath her, she dug her nails into her arm and the pain made her detach her mind and she slowed her breathing down, she would never let him go, she was Mrs Donnelly this was her home, no one was taking her place her name was all she had, she could feel the calm spreading through her body, she sat down and started to paint her face into the person she knew Adam would expect, thinking let's see what was so urgent and couldn't wait.......

Adam called Nancy and told her he was going to be home late, he had a few meetings that he needed to catch up on, Nancy didn't mind she knew she was with someone that definitely wasn't a nine to five guy, she was tired out and wanted a soak in the bath, a quiet night to recharge the batteries was on the cards for her. Adam made his way through the country lanes to Chigwell he marvelled at the beautiful houses that got bigger and spaced further apart as he drove along, he finally drove up to the electric gates of his house.

He loved this house when he bought it, it was a steal, now he looked at it differently as was no longer attached to it, he was willing to give Deb the house and a good settlement to set him free, he drove down the long drive to the house and parked up by the stables, the lights were on low and the door was already open Debbie was waiting on the doorstep for him for him, she looked like a painted porcelain doll, not one hair was out of place, not a crease to be seen on her silk pant suit "I was surprised when Mrs swan gave me the message that you were coming for dinner" she looked at him curiously, he looked different, he looked like a man who had a purpose, "come in lets go and sit down in the family room" the irony was not lost on either of them, as Debbie gracefully sat down, Adam sat opposite her and run his hand through his hair, "look Deb I'm here because I'm not waiting around anymore, you know were not happy and haven't been for some time, well let's be honest years, I have met someone else, and I want to be with her, Debbie I want a divorce" Debbie shook her head, "I will never divorce you Adam I am Mrs Donnelly" Adam jumped up out of the chair in frustration "I will give you the house and set you up for life, but this divorce is going to happen" she looked him and smiled not in the least bit bothered she sat back in her chair, "do you think it will be that easy Adam that I will let you just go and move on with your life? I will rip your life apart Adam, I will open you family business up like a cans of worms and" before she could finish her sentence Adam walked across the room and grabbed her out of her chair, "listen you stupid women it's over, we can do this two fucking ways, I will give you what you want and you will keep your mouth shut and move the fuck on or we can do this your way, and you will get nothing I will make sure that you will regret that choice so think very carefully" he held her in front of him, "it's over Debbie can't you see this is not right it's not healthy, I don't love you, and you don't love me it's over" all of this went straight over her head "who is she?" She asked softly "what has she got that I haven't" she had forgotten all the years of resentment and bitterness, this was a new feeling she could feel a cunning streak running through her body "it don't matter anymore Debbie but the paperwork is being filed and I want this divorce and one way or another it's going to happen, you have to think how you want this to end, because this is it Debbie it's the end" he let go of her and walked out of the living room. Adam had to walk away because he literally wanted to punch her to the ground to knock some sense into her. "Mrs swan I'm not stopping" Mrs swan was in the kitchen trying to pretend that she wasn't hanging off every word that Adam had said, she knew her days were numbered here, she had hung on for dear life but this was not the job for her, she was ready to move on she wanted a home with laughter and children to love, working for that frigid bitch in there was taking a toll on her, "ok my lovely you have a safe journey" she took the stew from the oven and placed it on the side as the front door slammed shut she walked into the living room, "would you like me to serve some dinner?" She was shocked at what she came across Mrs Donnelly was standing at the window watching Adam leave, she had a face that was pure evil, her makeup was smudged across her face and her hair was standing on end, she turned to Mrs swan and laughed manically "no dinner for me Mrs swan, did you hear that man, he honestly thinks it's going to be that easy" she laughed crazily her hands shaking as she poured herself a large scotch, she drunk it back in one gulp "I am going to turn in for the night" she picked the decanter up and walked up the stairs slowly Mrs swan watched her go, I will ring Mr Donnelly tomorrow and give my notice she felt uneasy in this house and had done for a long time, she had a terrible foreboding feeling that this was not going to be a happy ending for anyone.

The following morning Adam didn't tell Nancy that he had been to see Debbie the night before to discuss the divorce, the ball was now rolling and as far as he was concerned there was no turning back, he sat down eating toast and watched Nancy and Ronnie chattering away happily oblivious to the thoughts that were going through his head, he smiled as Nancy brought him over a cup of tea, he pinched her bum as she walked away, and gave her a saucy wink, "so Ron you done all your homework" she nodded and picked up her schoolbag she drunk her tea and put her cup in the sink "I'm going a school now aunty Sue is taking me as she wants to go to Watney market mum" Nancy nodded Ronnie walked up to Adam and kissed him on the cheek "have a good day", "you too sweetheart", he looked across at Nancy and she just stood there, she still had to pinch herself, Ronnie might not be Adam's child but he loved her like she was his own, Ronnie was a good girl. Nancy looked at Adam and said softly "any man can make a child but it takes a real one to be a father", her eyes welled up as she cleared the breakfast things away "I don't know what's come over me I am getting so soppy!" He laughed and walked up behind her, "I love you for it". I have a few meetings that will run late tonight do you want to ask Sue to have Ronnie and we have a late supper and go back to the flat in Wapping, she turned and looked at him flashing a smile, showing her bright white teeth, sounds good to me, he kissed Nancy slowly, looking forward to the night that stretched ahead.

As Adam and Nancy drove through the city it was already noon and the streets were busy, Nancy watched the world go by preoccupied with the bar, the drag night was such a success they were considering running it over the Friday and Saturday but that meant the girls were losing a night, the building next door had become available and she was thinking that maybe branching into both buildings and running two separate businesses, would be a better idea, they were obviously close enough that she keep a tight grip on them both and her attention could be split between them. Adam told her to talk to his brother Dennis he was the money man of the family, he was already looking at the lease and seeing if there was already room for movement, it would need a complete refurb but they had the boys that could do that, Adam was proud that Nancy had the same drive as him she as always looking for ways to improve the take and push the money further, all the family liked her, she went to every family celebration and dinner and was welcomed with open arms.

As they pulled up at the club Adam kissed Nancy on the cheek and she jumped out leaving behind the smell of her perfume in the car as a reminder, he drove off already thinking of the meetings he had planned for the day, as he pulled up at the offices, he walked through and greeted everyone with a friendly wave and walked slowly up the stairs to his office. Stevie was already in with a cup of tea in his hand, as he blew on the tea and reached for his rich tea, he looked up at his brother, and smiled "evening" "piss off" Adam shot back "we have our hands full today and we have been summoned to mothers for 7pm as well" Stevie was intrigued "well we better get cracking the boys up north want to push a new product they reckon it will be a money spinner, well set up the meet and let's see what they have on the cards" the day moved quickly. As they jumped into the jag Stevie was already looking forward to a bit of dinner round his mother's you was always guaranteed a hot plate when you walked in that house, it didn't matter what time it was Puna always had something on the go. As the brothers pulled up outside Spring Walk, Stevie locked the car up and they walked into Puna's, they were surprised to see Mary sitting up the table, the house was unusually quiet as the boys sat down, Puna pulled some plates of plates covered with tin foil that had been warming in the oven I made you some shepherd's pie, Mary I did you a plate as well, she looked at the plate hungrily "I'm not eating mum I'm meeting Nancy at the flat and were going out for a late supper", Puna smiled and put the extra plate in the oven no doubt one of the boys would turn up at some point and eat it. Stevie was eating his dinner with gusto when Adam turned to Mary and asked, "what can we do for you?" Mary smiled "no boys it's what I can do for you, I have a nice little earn for you boys and I want a serious drink from it" as she told her story she noticed both men had stopped moving and were now hanging on her every word, they asked about everything the security, what alarms did they have, the number of the safes and the housing of the safety deposit boxes. Mary pulled out her trump card that really knocked them for six, she pulled some old blueprints out of her bag she had stashed them away years ago no one even knew they existed and then she shared the final little piece of information that would pull them in on the job, there was a large safety deposit box that an old Russian had "he comes from the house of Oldenburg's that man has put some very nice Faberge eggs and tiaras in that box, he comes in once a year and pulls everything out, cleans it and then puts it back he has got a ruby in there that is the size of an egg I want to be able to retire somewhere nice and hot when the time comes boys and I know you will not turn me over so what do you say" Adams tea had gone cold a long time ago, he sat back in his chair thinking this was the golden goose sitting right here in front of him, he looked at Stevie who nodded, Adam smiled magnanimously "well I will have a meet with my brothers but I can tell you now the man from Delmonte he says yes" mum get the scotch out this deserves a toast! everyone laughed around the table, "now Mary tell me everything again" she smiled as they all leaned in to discuss the skull duggery at length.

Back at the club Nancy had a thumping head ache, girls fighting over johns was not the start to the day that she had envisioned and to top it off it had all unfolded in full view of the clientele on the floor not even out the back! A diabolical liberty as far as she was concerned and that see both girls getting sent home and suspended for a week, Nancy was firm but fair, these girls were greedy money hungry fuckers that had pushed it too far on this occasion. As she sat in her little private booth going over the books, Sandra walked over with a mug of steaming tea, Nancy went to take a mouthful and the smell hit her nostrils, she covered her mouth she had come over all nauseous, she jumped up and rushed to the toilet where she violently emptied the contents of her stomach, she walked out of the toilet shakily and wash her hands and patted her face, she looked positively green. She walked back to the table and sat down heavily her knees were knocking, Sandra eyed her up and jokily asked "you aren't up the club, are you?" Nancy laughed "behave yourself I must have eaten a dodgy Chinese last night" she smiled and pushed the tea away "bring me a glass of water Hun" smiling weakly. As Sandra walked away her heart sunk, she knew it wasn't food she had a cast iron stomach, years on the street taught her one thing she could eat a scabby horse and be as right as rain, trying to remember her last period, please god I can't be its probably a stomach bug making the rounds and brushed it off, she carried on finishing the books off and wrote a list for the bar manager to deal with before she left. Adam had rung and was on his way so she popped the takings in her bag and decided to bank the days takings in the night safe at the end of the road, as she walked out in to the evening air, she walked purposely to Barclays and deposited the takings unaware that she was being watched from a car that was parked up, as she walked back to the bar, Adam pulled up and she waved and she ran to the car and jumped in, she leaned across and kissed Adam on the lips, this little tableau was being observed and they were completely unaware," you ok girl" she smiled shakily you look a bit peaky, "I feel like I'm coming down with the flu babe shall we just have a night indoors" "of course how about I knock us up a bit of dinner" Nancy laughed "you, cook!" "I make a pukka bean on toast I'll let you know" "Sue has got Ronnie tonight so we will stay in the other flat ok" Nancy nodded glad as she was bone tired.

As they pulled away from the pavement and eased themselves into the night traffic they were still unaware that a few cars behind them was the car that had been watching them, they talked all the way back to the flat catching up on the day oblivious. Adam parked up and walked opened the door for Nancy to get out, she tucked her arm in his and they walked into the old warehouse together, the car had parked up and the occupant was silently watching, the driver looked up In the wing mirror and was surprised to see tears running silently down her face, Debbie now knew that Adam was lost to her, she had already found out about the women, and was shocked to see how close they were, Nancy was more beautiful in the flesh, her lip raised to a bitter sneer, a dirty brass had stolen her man, already her mind was ticking, the plans for revenge were already beginning to take shape, I am going to rip his heart out of his chest and shatter it into a million pieces.

Debbie drove home in such a rage she was surprised that she didn't lose control of the car and end up in a ditch, she knew there was someone else she wasn't stupid but since she started to wean herself off the pills she had a clarity that she had never had before. She walked into the house and walked to the study and unlocked it, she had all the locks changed the day Adam walked out of the house including the office, as she walked in and closed the door and flipped the lock she looked around, Debbie had already achieved so much in a short space of time, looking around she had files building on Adams businesses and pictures adorned the walls of the family, there were pictures of Nancy holding her daughters hand going to the shops, the kid was pretty and that burnt her even more, the whore could have kids, grabbing a pair of scissors she violently scratched Nancy out of the pictures, I'm going to ruin all your fucking lives and reduce you to ash, she sat in Adams chair and laughed pouring a large scotch she raised a glass to their picture, they had no idea what was coming all she had to do know was join the dots and laugh as she destroyed them all.

Adam was worried Nancy was not herself at all, she had definitely eaten something dodgy, she had been sick for three days before she finally given up and made an appointment to see the doctor she felt like death warmed up her eyes had shadows under them, she felt so weak, all she had to do was smell something and it set her off, tea her staple of life was now a no go she sat down heavily at Puna's and smiled, "blimey girl you look rough" Nancy grimaced "no tea for me have you got any lemonade" Puna smiled and pulled a bottle of R Whites out of the fridge. She poured her a glass and walked over to the table, as she put the glass down Nancy jumped up and went to get her bag "Adam wanted me to give you this key" as she rummaged in her bag as Puna lit a cigarette and sat back, she blew the smoke out slowly and looked at Nancy appraisingly even sick the girl was stunning," sit down sweetheart I want to have a chat with you it's just me and you today, what time is Adam picking you up?" Nancy sipped at her lemonade "His just popping to get Ronnie and were off us for dinner, he wants to take Ronnie to that Italian in Wapping she loves the spaghetti there" she smiled at the thought of Adam and Ronnie he spoilt her rotten "listen Nancy your 32 now aren't you?" Nancy nodded "sweetheart when was your last period?" Nancy felt the heat rising up her neck to her face, "were really careful" Nancy was mortified, Puna stretched her hands across the table and Nancy without hesitation placed her hands in hers, "darling your pregnant" "I can't be I've always been on the pill", even though she knew that was stretching the truth, since she had been with Adam half the time she forgot to take them that's why her periods had returned and were all over the place, "it happens I'm telling you your pregnant your boobs are bigger and you have that look I won't say nothing but I will lay money on it you are a few months along. Nancy was so shocked she just nodded, since she had met Adam she had laid off the coke and was only drinking wine with a meal, their sex life was explosive to say the least but surely it couldn't be true. "what am I going to do" she was petrified at the thought, Puna patted her hands "go to the doctors and take a test, mums the word, I won't repeat" Nancy wanted to cry she could feel the tears building "now don't get your knickers in a twist, you have us around you now girl and trust me if you are Adam will be over the moon, I will keep it all stoom, but get to that doctors pronto" Nancy nodded and pulled her hands away when she heard the door open, Ronnie come steaming in and threw her arms around Puna, who returned the hug with gusto she genuinely loved this little girl she was a little sweetheart, she looked over at Nancy and thought just like her mother, how she was going to keep quiet and not tell her sisters or the girls was going to be a killer, she prayed silently please god give my son a child he was born to be a father. Adam completely oblivious to the conversation smiled at Nancy "come on women get your bag, spaghetti is a waiting" Adam sung in a false Italian voice Ronnie laughed and picked up her things "come on mum I'm starving" Nancy kissed Puna on the cheek "I will pop in later this week for a bit of cake and a cuppa" Puna nodded "see you then darling" she followed them out and watched them both holding Ronnie's hand as they walked back to the car, she waved them off smiling, she turned and looked up at the sky and literally prayed please god give my boy another reason to get out of the bed in the morning.

"Well Nancy it looks like congratulations are in order" Nancy looked at the doctor so stunned she couldn't speak, "but doctor how? I'm on the pill!" still not admitting to herself that she hadn't taken her pill properly "It's very rare but it does happen, I'm going to send you to the London hospital for a scan" knowing Nancy's history he looked at her and asked gently "would you like me to arrange a termination" she shook her head, "no I'm keeping the baby" instinctively she put her hand protectively over her stomach this time it was different, this baby was made out of love, she had already come a long way with Ronnie, she knew that this time it was different, "well that's good you will need to make an appointment with the midwife when you go out to reception I'm going to take some blood now just to check your iron ok" Nancy was spiralling in shock, she was scared stiff how was Adam going to react?

Nancy kept the secret to herself and was in complete shock until a week later, she laid on the examination table and a sweet little West Indian midwife put the cold jelly on her lower abdomen and placed the scanner over her tummy straight away she could hear the babies heartbeat, the tears were now falling freely, "are you ok my lovely" the midwife asked, she nodded and watched the screen, "as you can see the baby is fine your about sixteen weeks along by the looks of things, would you like a picture?" Nancy nodded, the midwife smiled and put the paddle to the side of the machine and copied off a small picture of the baby, Nancy wiped her stomach with the blue paper towel and took the picture, looking down she smiled, there was no running away from this, but the funny thing was she didn't want to whatever happened she knew that this baby would be loved unconditionally, she was terrified at the prospect of telling Adam but she would face it all head on and they would work it out.

Adam was driving along frowning as he thought about Nancy she had become very quiet and distant, she didn't go to work today he was a bit taken a back as she didn't tell him, he popped in to see if she fancied a bit of late lunch and Sandra said she had booked the day, out since when did the staff no more about his Nancy then he did? he was driving down to his mums for a cuppa he had no secrets from her, he wanted to get to the bottom of this, he had a lot on his plate the brothers had to go over to Spain in the next week to see an old pal Freddie Price, he was an old jeweller out of Hoxton that was a good friend to their dad he could move all of the big items on and not even break a sweat, he didn't have to work anymore but he knew everyone, they were hoping to entice him out of retirement and take on this bit of graft Adam needed his contacts so was willing to sweeten the deal with a healthy cut, as far as he was concerned there was enough meat on the bone to keep everybody happy, Mary was already dreaming of sangria, he smiled wearily imagining Mary with a saucy waiter god help him. Adam parked up and quickly went into mums, "put that kettle on mum I'm gasping she put a cup out and poured him a tea from her pot that was permanently on the go" "here boy, what's up?" he run his hand through his hair "mum I'm fifty two now and feel like a bloody teenager you know I have only ever had Debbie as my serious relationship yes there has been other women but they were just flings, I have nothing to compare what me and Nancy have too, I love her mum there will never be no one else for me and that's the truth but something is off, she had gone quiet and that girl could have a fight with her own fingernails if she fancied it, I'm worried" Puna smiled at her boy, she knew Nancy's secret but couldn't tell him it was not her place, "listen boy that girl loves the bones of you, she isn't going anywhere, seeing you with her makes me so happy you wasted over twenty years of your life with a women that gave you nothing back, no love no life no children, don't give up on your Nancy the thing with that girl is no one has ever cared about her, she was treated like dirt for so long she forgot her worth boy and let me tell you she is a good match for you, she is loyal and will fight for you" her eyes misted over "I just wish you hadn't had to wait so long for the right girl to come along, she got up and walked around the table he stood up and walked into her embrace "you're never too old to have a cuddle from your old mum" he looked down at her what a women at 70 years old she was a marvel to everyone around her, "thanks mum" he said gruffly "I'm sure whatever will come out will be ok", "son in the end the truth always comes out" as he sat down she stood up and started to make him a sandwich she cut thick slices of bread, and pulled a plate of freshly cut ham out of the fridge she knew the ways to her boys heart, as she was making him a sandwich there was a knock on the door. Adam jumped up to answer it and Puna carried on buttering the bread, "hello babe what are you doing here?" he searched Nancy's face worried "I rung the office and Linda said you was coming here on your way home and I was in Whitechapel and thought I would walk over save me getting a cab back" as she walked through the hallway her face was flushed she locked eyes with Puna she had been struggling with this secret and keeping it from Adam was killing her, Puna knew straight away what was going down and was not missing one bit of this she placed the plates down on the table and poured Nancy a glass of lemonade from the fridge Nancy smiled up at her, she remembered, that simple act was her undoing, oh what she would do to have her mum with her, she was so lucky to have Puna on her side. Nancy looked at Adam and started to feel the hot salty tears falling down onto her cheeks she already looked a mess, Adams heart felt like it was being ripped out of his chest he couldn't bear to watch Nancy crying "please Nancy tell me what the fuck is wrong you haven't been right for a couple of weeks" Nancy looked at Puna who nodded "go on girl tell him" she held onto Adams hand and whispered "I'm pregnant" she looked down she was so scared to look into his eyes, "I'm just over four months I had it all confirmed today" she pulled the scan picture from her pocket and slid it across to Adam, "you're going to be a father" Adam looked at the picture in front of him, and picked it up he was shaking so bad he could not hold it straight, he couldn't breathe he was so shocked he just stared at the picture I'm having a baby! he touched his face and looked at his hand, to his shock he was crying Adam Donnelly was crying like a baby, he kicked the chair out from under him and scooped Nancy up in his arms crying real tears they were both crying together holding her to face him in his arms he looked at her "for twenty years all I have ever wanted was my own family, a child, and all I got was an empty shell you have walked into my life and turned everything on its head, Nancy I love you, you're the love of my life and you have given me the one thing money couldn't buy, a baby" Puna stood there her hands on her mouth silently crying taking in the love and raw emotion that was pouring out around her table, "Nancy we are going to get married I am going to adopt Ronnie and we are going to raise our family we have a shot at a fresh start a new beginning, you are my life" he was kissing her fingers crying he was completely stunned, Puna rushed to them and put her arms around them, finally! If she was taken from the earth today, she would sleep the sleep and rest easy knowing finally her boy would have the family he deserved. as they calmed down Puna said "so please tell me can I call the family" Nancy looked at Adam and smiled he laughed "go on then mother get on the blower and get everyone round tell Stevie to pick Ronnie up from Sues let's tell everyone together"

Two hours later the house was fit to burst as soon as Puna got on the blower the bongo drums were well and truly beating even Puna's sisters were there, Adam looked around and smiled it was standing room only he looked at them all with love, that was the one thing about his family if you needed them they were there in a heartbeat, he put his fingers in his mouth and whistled to grab their attention, they all stopped talking and looked at him expectantly, he winked at his mum "nice to see you all here tonight" "get on with it" Stevie shouted from the sofa, Adam put his hands up in mock surrender "ok I will get on with it" Ronnie was standing next to her beloved Puna who had her arm around her shoulders, "we wanted you all here tonight so we could tell you the good news I have waited a very long time for this moment, I'm going to be a father" the whole place erupted everyone was up out of their chairs at once kissing and hugging Nancy and Adam, Puna already had bottles of champagne on ice out in the garden and got the boys to start passing the buckets in, it was complete bedlam, no one could believe it finally Adam was going to be a father, Stevie was shaking his hand so hard his teeth were shaking he laughed and hugged his brothers one after the other, his sisters all embraced Nancy she was truly now one of them, he put his arm out to Nancy and Ronnie and pulled them both close, everyone raised their glasses, Dennis shouted "cheers! To Adam and Nancy" everyone raised their glasses smiling from ear to ear "to Adam and Nancy" they toasted the first glass of many.

Chapter seven

Everything was moving fast, Nancy refused point blank to give up work, so he moved big Dave to her side and pulled some new boys onto the door, Dave sat at the side of her booth positioned by the bar and he never left her side, he took the responsibility of watching over Adams precious cargo very seriously, not very many people knew the history of these two men but they had each other's backs and Dave knew for Adam to entrust Nancy and the baby to him was the highest form of respect that his good friend could give him, he had grown to love Nancy like she was like his little sister, she had a heart of gold and as he proudly told anyone more balls then John Barnes.

"Babe seriously I have got your passport come over to Mercia with me and Stevie we are meeting up with an old friend of the family and then we can have a couple of days together out there" Nancy shook her head stubbornly "no I'm going to stay here we have booked some headliners in the bar and I want to make sure it all goes off right" at five and a half month pregnant everything had moved so fast, Adam had taken the bar over next door to the one he already had and it ripped out in record time, his boys refurbished it and put in a bigger stage, the drag acts were a major pull to the punters and it had become a bigger success then they both envisioned. Nancy was showing and Adam didn't like to leave her alone, in fact he didn't like leaving her full stop, he had already put all the paper work in for the divorce not that he was having much luck with Debbie he frowned at the thought of her, she had banned him from the house not that he give a shit that was a relief to be honest, but she had not replied to any of the correspondence sent to her. Adam already knew that Mrs Swan had left, but he had a surprise up his sleeve for Nancy two more weeks and whether she liked it or not they were moving out of this flat, he smiled at the thought of the house he had bought for them to move into, Mrs swan was going to take over as housekeeper,

Nancy had already met her for lunch after she had left Debbie's employment and they had hit it off straight away, he walked up behind Nancy and placed his hands on the belly, "the baby's cooking good in there" she laughed, "you know we can find out the sex of the baby if you want and you can be put out of your misery" "no I want the surprise, Nancy I have waited a long time for this baby so I'm happy, as long as the baby and you are healthy that's enough for me" he kissed her on her neck, "come on hurry up let's get to work I have got a full day and so do you" she pulled at his shirt hem, he looked at her with a raised eyebrow Nancy purred "I'm sure they wouldn't mind if you was a little late" as he looked into her eyes his lips inches above hers, "what do you have in mind" he replied huskily, "oh you have no idea" as she walked him into the bedroom.

Making love to Nancy had taken on a new meaning to Adam, it was now something deeper and they both knew it, they both had an insatiable appetite for each other's bodies, he had thought that Nancy being pregnant would slow them down it had been the opposite, he was in awe at the charges in her blossoming body he stared at her in wonder, he already had a ring in the safe waiting for the house to be finished, in two weeks he was going to propose he was not waiting any longer he wanted her to know that he intended on marrying her, she had given him everything he had ever wished for and he wanted to give her the world, he bent down and kissed her gently on the lips "you lady are my life" she smiled back up at him and replied "and you are mine"

Adam dropped Nancy at the curb and kissed her on the lips "I will pick you up later and we will go and have a late supper, Sue has got Ronnie so we don't have to rush back" "ok babe" Dave came out of the club and walked towards the car, he spotted a car pull in a few cars back he caught a glimpse but couldn't see the driver properly but there was something familiar about her, he squinted in the sun but got distracted by Nancy opening the door, he put his hand out protectively to her, she turned and waved Adam off and they walked in to the club together. Little did they realise that sitting behind them was Debbie, she was sitting in the car gripping the wheel her breathing was laboured she thought she was going to black out, she tried to calm herself down but was in absolute shock the whore was pregnant this changed everything. I'm going to kill her I am going to wipe her off the face of the earth she was wildly ranting to herself.

Debbie pulled away from the pavement and drove quickly through the city traffic, she needed to get home, she needed to get in her house and close the door she could hear her heart beating in her ear drums as she drove through Chigwell she pressed the button for the electric gates to slide open and drove quickly down the drive pulling the car into the garage she quickly pulled the garage door down and walked into the house through the side door, she threw the keys onto the side in the kitchen and poured a large glass of scotch into a cup, and drank it back quickly, refilled her glass and repeated this until she could feel her heart beat slowing down and her body loosening up. Debbie looked around, well the house had certainly changed since Mrs

Swan had left, dishes were piled up in the sink and left abandoned on the sides in the kitchen, there was bags of rubbish piled up by the back door the smell of ripe rubbish was an assault to the senses not that she could smell or see any of it, the house was grimy thick with dust. She looked across to the garden and started to laugh, the scorched grass was the only reminder of the bonfire she had lit, every picture and item of clothing that belonged to Adam had been burnt on the front lawn a drop of petrol and it went up lovely! Debbie kicked her shoes off her feet sticking to the kitchen floor and walked to the office, she smiled at the progress she had made, it was amazing what money could buy, she had already amassed a shocking amount of information about Adam, the whore and his family, she decided to move it up a gear now seeing as the bitch was pregnant she went to the drawer and pulled her new passport out, and tapped it purposely on the desk yes a little trip to Marbella was definitely now on the cards it was time to find Billy the final piece in the puzzle when it came to her plans of revenge, she knew he definitely had a score to settle.

Adam kissed Nancy again "for the last time are you sure you're going to be ok" she laughed "for the final time I'm fine! Now get a move on you have to be at the airport in three hours, Gatwick is a hard drive in the rush hour so get a wiggle on" he kissed her again and picked up his bag "I will be back in a couple of days ok" with that he was gone all that he had left behind was the smell of the aftershave that little Ronnie had bought him for his birthday, he wore it with pride. As he jumped in the back of the car Stevie was reading the paper they made their way to the airport cutting in and out of traffic young Glen drove like a rocket down the motorway, as they jumped out Adam was actually happy to get out in one piece, "I tell you what I will keep him in mind for any high risk driving jobs he would make a good getaway driver" Stevie chuckled as they walked in and booked in their cases in and sat in the business lounge waiting to board, little did they realise another person was walking through the sliding doors of Gatwick with an equal amount of purpose. Debbie booked in her case and waited to board to go to Marbella she already had an address and his whereabouts committed to memory she wasn't willing to take no for an answer, as both partners boarded their flights, and went to their destinations neither were aware of how close they had come to bumping into each other.

The first thing Debbie felt when the door opened on the aeroplane was the humidity it hit her like a slap in the face her clothes were stuck to her body, if it was already this hot in June I wouldn't be able to handle the heat in the height of the summer, this was the first time that Debbie had travelled on a plane in fact the only place she had ever been too away from home was Bournemouth on her honeymoon, her lip raised at the thought of her honeymoon she scorned her past, she was doing a lot of things she had never imagined in the name of revenge. She walked through the terminal and hailed a taxi; she gave the driver the address of the villa and sat back and watched the scenery as the vehicle made its way through the streets. Debbie had rented close to the bars that Billy frequented she wanted privacy everything had been planned down to the finest detail.

As the cab pulled up she was greeted by the agent with the keys, she walked around the traditional Spanish villa and was surprised how pretty it was, Adam had property's all around the world, he had often asked her to go to Spain and she had always declined she regretted that as it was a beautiful Country. As she walked into the cool shade she kicked off her shoes and walked across the cold marble tiles that run throughout the property, she opened the fridge and pulled a bottle of wine out and poured herself a glass of crisp white wine, everything she had requested was done, it was amazing what you could do when you had the means, she walked up the stairs taking a sip from the glass she looked around the beautiful white washed bedrooms, the shuttered windows were pushed open and the breeze was gently blowing the voile curtains, she walked onto the balcony and stopped in her tracks, the unparalleled view of the sea and lush landscape was simple breath-taking she stood there drinking her wine unwinding and planning out what laid ahead, she knew that the key to destroying Adam laid with Billy and she was not prepared to take no for an answer. Debbie showered and dressed carefully she applied light make up as she already had a glow just from sitting on the balcony on in the late sun, she had made a reservation at a restaurant that Billy owned and knew this would be the place where she would make contact, she looked good and she knew it, she walked out of the villa and took the short walk to the beach front. She could hear the Frank Sinatra singer crooning away at Billy's steak and lobster restaurant and was surprised to see how busy it was, she walked in and sat herself at the bar and ordered a glass of champagne she turned her bar stool round so she had a clear view of the restaurant, she spotted Billy straight away, he was walking through the bar stopping at tables being the congenial host smiling and laughing.

Billy wore his shirt opened at the neck to show off his deep tan, he looked up and locked eyes with Debbie and felt the pull of her, as he made his way between the tables towards her, he smiled, she returned the smile while sipping on her champagne, "I'm sorry you look so familiar to me but I can't place your face" she laughed she put out her hand and he immediately gripped it, "I'm Debbie and your Billy" he looked at her still unsure of what to say she had his attention, "I'm Adam Donnelly's wife" Billy froze and pulled his hand away, "don't worry his not here, we are separated as you well know his been fucking one of your brasses Nancy" his eyes dilated in shock at the coarse language coming from such a posh mouth, he was intrigued, Billy smiled "come lets go and sit somewhere a little more private and you must try the lobster here" Debbie followed him to his private table and sat down opposite him, "I'm not going to beat around the bush with you Billy I have flown here because we have both been mugged off by Adam and that slag of a women and I want to pay them back in spades, now I thought that seeing as you lost so much and had to wipe your mouth and walk away you would want a in on this" She looked across the table at Billy who sat back in his chair, he clicked his fingers at the waiter "Miguel bring me a bottle of our best champagne on ice over and we will have the lobster" he waited as the waiter brought over the bucket filled with ice and Dom

Perignon, he nodded as he popped the cork and theatrically filled the fresh flutes. As the server walked away Billy raised his glass "you have no idea how I have waited for this moment" Debbie smiled in relief, she raised her glass and top a sip, they then got down to the serious business of the matter at hand, as the night moved along Debbie realised that Billy had a nice face but wasn't the sharpest tool in the box, but as she smugly told herself that made it easier for her to manipulate him, they had made short work of the champagne and were now drinking large brandy's, she stretched out already satisfied with how the evening had gone so well to plan, "I have rented a villa a stone's throw away from here, she gave him the address, come over for lunch tomorrow so we continue this" he tucked the card in his top pocket and smiled, "I'll be there".

On the other side of the sunny island, Adam was sitting across the table with his brother, laughing while drinking a cup of tea, Freddie was loving the boxes of PG Tips and frozen bacon, good old Puna had packed him a box of goodies that you just couldn't get over in Spain that was the only thing he missed his tea bags and bacon, "so boys what's the rub" Freddie looked at them with the glint in his eye he was officially out of the game, but these boys held a special place in his heart, he was best friends with their dad and had seen how the family operated, there was no outsiders and no treachery and he liked how they weren't greedy, he had a lot of respect and love for them and it showed "We have a job that is going to need some serious movement there are some serious big ticket items and we are only going ahead if you are on board, it's a family operation as always and the we are ready, this will set you and your family up, so what do you think Uncle?" they told him a quick breakdown of the graft ahead and looked at him expectantly, they used the term Uncle with Freddie because that's how they saw him, he was a constant in their lives growing up, Freddie blew on his tea and looked around the beautiful villa and sparkling pool, "boys I don't need the money I have enough to see me through ten times over, but I love the life and I'm bored shitless so count me in" the boys were made up it was now all systems go, Freddie leaned in and spoke quietly "now tell me I heard you right there's a ruby the size of my balls on the table?" the boys roared with laughter, they leaned in and smiled "oh yes Uncle and some Faberge eggs" Freddie's brain was already ticking he already had people in mind for the ruby and eggs that would pay top whack, "boys go get my good cigars because I think we're going to have a very good year" the boys looked at each other laughing, it's on!

The brothers spent a further couple of days with Freddie he was a real blast and was happy to have the boys over, they went out for a couple of meals together Freddie knew it was always nice to remind the other ex-pats that he was a force to be reckoned with and had major backing not that he give a shit but it sure made his paella go down a treat seeing the look on some of the youngers faces when they clocked who he was sitting with. Having a new earn on the horizon had given him the little kick that he needed there was nothing better than growing old disgracefully, he had already lined the eggs up to go to a good friend in Saudi Arabia and the ruby was being moved onto to a very influential man in japan, the boys were finishing their paella, they had loved spending time with their Uncle, he regaled them with stories of the past and their father who they deeply missed, but they had a flight to catch tonight and Adam was chomping at the bit to get home and put everything into action and see his Nancy, the boys had rung and the house was nearly finished which proved if you bung a few quid in the right direction anything was possible he had bought a massive Georgian house in Holland park, Kensington and it was absolutely stunning, he had kept all the original features but had upgraded all of the bathrooms and had a state of the art kitchen installed to keep Mrs Swan happy, he had also inherited a beautiful garden that was a well-established haven, he had installed a children's play area, he wanted kids, plural and was hoping to fill the house with as many arms and legs possible, the place was being furnished by an interior designer that had the brief of family, classy and not to overpowering so far it was looking good.

Adam had decided to bring the proposal forward he didn't want to wait anymore and had also decided to meet with Debbie's solicitors he didn't give a fuck he wanted this sorted and cut and dried so he could marry his Nancy, he was packed and ready to go in no time, the chauffeur came to collect them as they were saying their goodbyes to Freddie, "we will be in touch" he shook their hands and hugged them goodbye, he was looking forward to the next few months nothing like being in the thick of it.

Debbie was looking at her complexion in the mirror a day in the sun had done wonders, she had well and truly reeled Billy in she was actually surprised at how quickly he agreed to get involved, the hatred he had for Adam and Nancy matched her own it was a heady combination. Debbie had held back telling him that Nancy was pregnant, some men would baulk at the idea of going after a pregnant women as it went against the old school rules of no women or children, but she knew that Billy was a spiteful fucker to his women so striping that bitches face was not going to be a problem for him, but if he knew she was pregnant he might hesitate and she didn't have time for anyone holding back, she wanted to rip Adams heart out of his chest and serve it to him on a platter and Nancy was the key to that. Billy was coming over for dinner tonight and she was going to ensure she pulled out all the stops before she left to ensure his loyalty, she had ordered in some food from the local restaurant and had the wines and champagne chilling she had a few glasses to desensitize herself, she knew what she had to do, Billy would see this as one up on Adam, whereas Debbie see this as pulling Billy close, she needed his backup for the final part of her plan and she was willing to do whatever it took to make sure she got him.

Billy arrived promptly and remarked on how good Debbie looked the sunshine definitely agreed with her, she was glowing, he had already decided to go back the England at some point so now they just had to go over the finer points, she had already told him she had gone into the Donnelly's business dealings and had amassed a lot of information on them, Billy could see that this was the opportunity that he needed, to get his foot back in and pay the Donnelly's back in spades he was relishing the look on Nancy's face, he rubbed his hands together with what he had planned for her. Debbie was in her forty's but had aged well, he had already decided to take one for the team and give her one, he could not wait to throw that one out there that he had fucked Adams Donnelly's wife, he was definitely going to milk this situation for all it was worth, the food was good the drinks were flowing and he could definitely feel a shift in the atmosphere between them it, he placed his glass down and cleared his throat "do you fancy a swim" Debbie looked across the table with her eyebrow raised, this could be more interesting than she thought, she stood up from the table and slowly walked towards the pool, she slipped her dress over her shoulders and discarded it on the floor, she was already completely naked underneath and she had drunk enough to drown out the shyness, she realised the only man she had every slept with was Adam, and it had been a very long time since they had been intimate.

Billy sat and watched Debbie as she slowly stripped her dress off he had to tip his hat to her she didn't have an inch of fat on her body, he slowly unbuttoned his shirt and stripped off, walking towards her he was already erect and ready for action, he was tanned all over, he held her hand and drew it down to his pulsating member and she started to slowly stroke him, he run his hands down from her breasts and slipped his hand between her legs slipping his fingers into her, she didn't do it for him he liked a curvy women, he was more turned on by the idea of the conquest, he was fucking a Donnelly's wife, he took his hand away and placed his fingers in her mouth, she sucked on his fingers and then gave him a deep kiss he could taste her and that exited him. He took her hand and led her slowly into the pool, he pushed her gently up against the wall and lifted her and entered her with one smooth swoop, she wrapped her legs around his body as he started to pound into her body, she arched her back as the sensation of the friction and water hit her body, her breasts bouncing, billy looked down at her and wanted to fuck her so hard that when she got up the next day she would still feel him on her body he twisted his body that was still locked in hers and laid her on the steps that walked into the pool and pushed into her further it was not enough, he wanted more so he quickly flipped her over so she was on her knees on the steps and he stood on the pool floor and took her from behind he was now pushing into her and going deeper, he could feel the rhythm take over his body and knew this was going to be quick, Debbie had already detached herself underneath him and was focusing on the plan at hand that's what got her exited not this mug that was trying to ride her like a pony above her. Billy was grunting loudly, she could feel him thickening inside her and readied herself, he pushed into her hard and orgasmed inside her, he slumped onto her back "that was magic" she nodded in agreement stifling a yawn, he pulled out of her, Debbie straightened up and silently walked from the pool, there was an outside shower, so she walked to it and started to shower herself down, Billy walked towards her "do you mind if I join you" she moved to one side and handed him scented gel that she had lathered her body with, as he watched her soap he body he felt himself stirring again, he pressed himself against her smiling, he had had a couple of lines of coke before dinner and he was now flying, she smiled over her shoulder "again?" he laughed bent her over and pushed himself into her, the buzz of the conquest had not worn off and he was going to fuck this women's body until she was raw.

Billy left the following morning, high on adrenaline, he whistled happily as he buttoned his shirt, he had rode her hard the final time, the hatred he felt for Nancy was spewing out of his body and he knew he had probably hurt Debbie but he didn't feel a flicker of shame, she took it and had come back for more, there was nothing better than a revenge fuck, it had proper got his juices flowing, they had agreed that he would be over in four weeks, he had plans to put into place and that would give him the time he needed, Debbie had agreed and knew they would remain in constant contact until he got back into the Britain.

Adam had hit the ground running as soon as he landed he went to the new house in Holland park, he could not believe the progress the house was literally ready to move into, he had planned everything for the big night, the garden was going to be covered in candles, he had also arranged for the caterers to set up a running buffet and bar, he smiled thinking about how the neighbours would take his lot pulling up outside, tomorrow night he was bringing Nancy and Ronnie to the house it was time and he was ready.

He made his way back to Bethnal green like a homing pigeon, he waved to Sue as he pulled up and threw her a duty-free bag containing eight hundred menthols, he knew the way to her heart. Adam ran up into the flat, Nancy was waiting for him, she flew into his arms, she was feeling emotional, being away from Adam when she was hormonal was a revelation to her, she had cried every night like a complete wally for a reason she couldn't even fathom all she knew was she didn't want Adam leaving her again, she knew Glen or Shaine were still stationed downstairs when Adam was not there but she had such a horrible foreboding feeling she couldn't shake it off "did everything go alright" Adam pulled her close to him and stroked her stomach she looked up at him her eyes were welling up "don't leave me again until the baby Is born" he nodded choked up, he realised he would have to box clever with the planning for Hatton garden and not stray too far from home, it was going to be hard graft but to keep the home happy he would do what he had to do "Do you want to go out for a bit of dinner or do you want a night in" she looked up her eyes dilating, I was hoping for an early night, he held her hand and led the way "well you're in luck lady as today I'm taking requests".

Later that night they lay in bed together, telling each other silly stories laughing, Adam was in awe the baby was obviously a night owl, and was kicking away happily, he kissed her soft belly gently, "I can't be without you Nancy you and the kids are my life" she snuggled into his arms and finally she was sound asleep he watch her breathing and stroked her belly, thankful for his blessings. Adam's brain couldn't switch off as he had serious work to deal with he was still awake wrapped around Nancy when the sun come up the following morning, he kissed her gently on the face and she opened one eye sleepily mumbling something that needed an interpreter to understand," listen I have got a lot on today, but I will be home before seven to pick you and Ronnie up, were going up west for a slap up meal so make sure your glammed up" she laughed "err hello I look like I'm carrying a baby buffalo" "Don't be silly you could dress up in a black bag and look the nuts, just be ready, I have made reservations"

Adam drove to work quickly and was glad to see all the boys were already waiting for him in the boardroom, the boys shut the doors behind him and took their seats "Firstly you know the score tonight, be at the new gaff before seven and try and keep the noise down for fucks sake your gobs will let the cat out the bag" they laughed, "now let's get down to business" "Freddie is on board and has already got buyers for the big ticket items, all the loose gold will be melted down once the stones have been removed, now we have the transport lined up and ready and the blueprints show us the weakest point to go through now remember we will be transporting everything through the sewage tunnels, it will be pumped up through the sewage truck here" Adam pointed at the map "we have the keys, we have the alarm codes we have everything set in place, the sewage truck is to be driven into Dartford docks, it will be put straight into a container" he nodded "Stevie has taken care of the port authority side, it was well handy that young Paul was slipped into the offices a few years ago he has everything covered there and it will be shipped straight to Spain, we have one of our boys going over with the container where it will be met, Freddie has taken care of the Spanish side" he looked around the table as he continued "Freddie has a farm up in the hills and it will be taken there, he has the furnace set up and ready to go, me and Stevie will go out for the final push and the money will be wired straight into the accounts in Zurich upon delivery, Brian tell me about the police" Brian give him the low down on the response time if the alarms were triggered "Dennis has all the paperwork gone in for the sewage works to be carried out?" "yep the City of London has issued the work orders to be carried out early Sunday morning we have a six hour window to get in and out" "right we are going to do some dry runs, Nathen has knocked up a portacabin in one of the yards like for like, safety deposit boxes and safe, were taking the lot everything has to be double bagged and cable tied we have 3 weeks to perfect this boys, so tell the wives and girlfriends that you will be working late until we have this sorted, I want this to run like a well-oiled machine or were not doing it at all, agreed?" they all nodded their heads "this is going to set us up for lives boys, this is a serious amount of graft were about to pull, we start tomorrow"

Everyone knew what part they had to play and took it seriously that's why they were successful the power and strength was always in their numbers, "right go on fuck off the lot of you, I will see you all later tonight" As they got up and left the room Stevie stayed seated and waited to have a word with Adam, "so what do you think?" "I think if we pull this off bruv were fucking magicians" Adam chuckled "you scared?" Stevie laughed "no chance you know me I love the challenge we have pulled faster strokes then this brother but this is the biggest, no one realised that you have had people greased into every aspect of planning, the ports or police for years just waiting for the opportunity to arise well now these fuckers are going to have to earn their keep" "no one outside the family knew about what was planned but everyone will get their taste brother you know me and that's what keeps their lips sealed" Stevie nodded sagely "it sure does"

Adam was busy for the rest of the day taking care of the arrangements for Holland park and having meetings with some of the boys, luckily every brother took care of a certain part of the business, so he didn't have to be so hands on anymore. He still liked to keep himself involved just to make sure no one fucked up, Linda was sitting at the desk typing away she didn't look up as she announced "Adam, Patsy the ring man is here for you" Adam stood up and walked around his desk as Patsy walked in he reached out and shook his hand "bloody hell what are you doing here?" "Freddie rung me, he knew I was making the ring up for your Nancy and he wanted me to give you a little gift that he had punted away a few years ago" Patsy took the box from his inside pocket and opened it, Adam was used to diamonds but this ring was another level, "it's a Graff Six carat pure white stone it is set with another two carats around the main stone, it has no inclusions this ring is the best of the best it's an old cut, you will never see another like this" Adam took the box and watched the brilliant sparkle as the light hit it, he didn't know what to say "it's a gift son, he knew you was going to propose and wanted you to have it" Adam was genuinely choked this was Freddie all over "thanks patsy" he put his hand on his shoulder, it probably cost more than the house he just bought! Patsy smiled and shook his hand; Adam sat down and placed the open box on the desk and rung Freddie he was blown away. Linda come in as ever wanting to know what the gossip was and let out a low whistle when she saw the ring sparkling on the desk, "dare I ask?" "Freddie sent it for Nancy" she shook her head not in the least bit surprised, he was a boy that Freddie.

Adam had a shower at the office and changed into a fresh suit and shirt, he made his way back to Bethnal green to pick up his girls. As he pulled up Nancy and Ronnie walked out of Sues, they looked a picture, Ronnie had on a lovely party dress and her hair shone in the late sun, he looked at his Nancy she was coming up to seven months and still managed to look gorgeous her eyes were sparkling she was positively blooming, Sue stood in the door way and waved them off, they all looked smashing, she couldn't wait for little Ronnie to get back and fill her in. Adam got the girls in the car and started making his way back through the city he was starting to feel it now, the adrenalin and nerves were starting to kick in. As they drove through Kensington Nancy started to smell a rat, they passed beautiful Georgian three story houses with black cast iron railings and white stone steps, "where's the restaurant?" "Were nearly here" Adam pulled outside a house and she looked at him, "have you got to stop off, babe I'm starving" "I want to show you something before we go for food indulge me babe we will be five minutes tops" Adam jumped out of the car, Nancy looked around and see the large communal gardens that the houses shared in the square that surrounded it, it had beautiful, well-aged trees and a grassed area with benches dotted here and there, it was immaculately kept. Adam started guiding Ronnie and Nancy towards the house they had parked outside of, he guided her up the steps, and took a set of keys out of his pocket and she looked up at him "what are you up to?" "come in and have a look" as he opened the door onto a grand large hallway, she could smell the fresh paint the floor was tiled with in black and white stone squares and the ceilings were high with the originally coving the stairs has a thick cream carpet going up the middle with gold rods to hold it securely in place "come and have a look around" he whispered gently into her ear, taking her hand he took her into the large living room, the windows had heavy curtains pulled back she looked out of the window and see the beautiful gardens, it was a lovely home, it had calming feeling to it, "let me show you the kitchen before we leave" Nancy muttered sarcastically "any chance we can knock up a sandwich" he laughed and pinched her bottom gently "come on happy chops" she followed him through to a large open plan kitchen, it was old house and the kitchen was brand new but sympathetic to the home it was put in what amazed her was there was a large open plan extension, she could see lights twinkling and flickering in the garden she sniffed the air "Adam I swear someone must have a BBQ going I can smell food" he walked towards the back door and slid the doors open, she held her breath in shock there was a huge amount of food all laid out a bar and what looked like massive BBQ's "I know I'm eating for two but come on I can't eat all that" as she turned back to Adam her hand flew to her mouth, Adam was down on one knee, "I waited twenty years for you to walk into my life, from the moment I saw you I knew you was the one that I was going to grow old with, you are my life Nancy, you have given me the gift that I have prayed for and that is a family, please will you marry me" he opened the blue velvet box, Nancy went weak at the knees sitting nestled in the velvet shining like fire was the most beautiful ring she had ever seen the stone was massive! "Ronnie what do you think my darling what should your mum say?" Ronnie couldn't even speak, the tears were rolling down her dear little face, she went to her mums side and hugged her tight, Nancy looked down at this man that had changed her life forever crying she nodded yes. Adam took the ring from the box and slid it on her finger "I promise you Nancy you will never be alone, I will love you and protect you until the day I die" he bent down and kissed her on the lips gently he then turned his attention to Ronnie, and pulled a little box out of his pocket and opened it, inside lay a diamond love heart on a chain with four little diamonds in "one for each of us my darling" as he was placing it round her neck, he looked at them both, "this is our new home, I want us to raise our family here, safely, what do you say?" they looked up at the back of the house and laughed when they noticed the family with their noses pressed on the glass watching everything unfold "how did you manage to keep that lot quiet" she laughed "you have no idea he replied dryly" As everyone rushed downstairs and congratulated him, the celebrations truly begun, he smiled as he watched his family around the garden Nancy was surrounded by his mum and sisters who were all inspecting the ring while Puna rubbed her belly Nancy laughed and kissed her mother in law to be "I do love you" and they embraced, he looked across at Ronnie who was happily playing on the swings with her cousins, Adam thought he was heart was going to explode in his chest he truly was a lucky man.

The following day they went back to Holland park so Nancy could see the house in the daylight and she was genuinely blown away, the house was over 3 floors and had multiple bedrooms and toilets, as she walked in she could smell breakfast and coffee, she looked at Adam and he winked, she walked through to the kitchen and to her shock Mrs swan was there "I thought I would give the kitchen a test drive my lovely's your just in time, take a seat and I will plate your breakfast up" Nancy looked at Adam shocked, but the smell soon distracted her, she tucked into the breakfast hungrily and sipped on the freshly made coffee, she looked around the sparkling kitchen, "so does Mrs Swan come with the house then?" "Well she left Debbie's a while ago she wasn't happy and I was hoping she would come in handy, she can take the pressure off the day to day running, she is a superb housekeeper, and she wants a family to look after" she nodded "it feels weird because I know she has worked with Debbie for years as long as she respects the fact that the women's name is never mentioned in this house that's fine" he laughed "there's no chance of that, I just want the papers signed then I can't get you up the aisle" Nancy blushed as she looked down at her ring "so where is Mrs swan going to stay?" "there's staff quarters in the basement she is already settled in and ready to go so what do you say shall we moved in?" she leaned over and kissed his nose "yes let's do it" Adam was over the moon "look the next few weeks are going to be hectic, so we will go back and forward I have a big job on as soon as its done we will settle in ok" he stroked her belly "can you believe you only have six weeks to go where has the time gone" the baby was kicking away happily, "were on the home stretch, now remember in the next few weeks I'm going to be working long hours babe, but you will have Glen downstairs, Dave will be your right hand man in the bar, and mother and the girls are around you" she raised her hand and stopped him in mid-sentence "your all suffocating me, I love you but I'm ok, if I need help I promise I will ask for it" he sighed "just humour me babe, you know I don't like to be away from you this way I can focus on the job at hand and not be dropping the ball" Nancy relented when she see the concern on his face "ok to keep the peace I will do what you want ok" he kissed her "see that wasn't hard was it" and laughed "come on let's get you to work, big Dave will be having kittens wondering where you are"

Chapter eight

Adam was in one of the old yards that they owned in the back of Chelmsford, it was set in acres of land and was very private, they had large barns that Ronnie the tan cultivated large quantities of cannabis, Ronnie was a permanent shade of mahogany and loved his all year tan, he ran the multiple sunbed shops across Essex that the Donnelly's owned but he loved to grow weed that was his forte, the boys payed him some serious wedge to grow the plants and the factory's were a serious earner. "So everything is set for two weeks Sunday, we are going through the sewers and smashing through the downstairs toilets pipeline all of the goods will be transported through these bags that are to be cable tied up, we have the correct work permits so the boys will have the truck looking like its pumping up sledge when it will be pumping up the graft, the alarms and safe will be opened by Bobby" they all laughed Bobby was being dressed up as an old orthodox Jew, seeing as the diamond district was predominantly Jewish they knew he would slip in unnoticed. "The alarms and keys have all been supplied by Mary, she had keys cut years ago and they haven't got a fucking clue, once the alarms have been deactivated Bobby will walk out the front and lock up jump on the tube to Bethnal green and be picked up by the boys he will be ready for the truck to be driven straight into a container that's being shipped over to Spain" he took a sip of his tea as he continued "me and Stevie are staying put because when this kicks off the police are going to spin everyone's homes and businesses so this load of skunk is going to be cut down dried and moved quickly all of the lighting will be taken down and stored in one of the old lock ups that are not related to us and when it calms down we will re set the grows up we have had a few dry runs and everything is looking good" Stevie laughed as he bit into his ham and pickle sandwich "luckily the old sewage tunnels that run under Hatton gardens were so close to the toilet block the walls would be cut through like a hot knife through butter, the boys had been pumping shit up through the drain and the shops have been chewing the city's earholes all week, we have had one of our men go in inspect the drains and say that there's a pipe that needs to be replaced, how fucking good is it we have City of London paperwork to rob Hatton garden" all the boys cracked up laughing, "keep gloved up, no prints, stay focused, no smoking as forensics is so good now they can DNA of a cigarette butts, once the graft is broken down it will take 12 weeks before the money starts to filter back to us, everyone will get their cut but NO one is to spend a penny that they cannot afford outside their wage bracket, we want no attention we are playing the long game you tell the wives that you a serious win down the casinos, our strength is because we stick together" he looked around the table at his brothers who all nodded in agreement, he knew they were going to pull of one of crimes of the century and it was going to make them, he was chomping at the bit, he loved a good old fashion robbery!

The next two weeks were a complete blur, late nights were the norm and any problems had to smoothed over quickly, and double checked as there was no room for error. The everyday operations still had to also have the families full attention and Adam also tried his upmost to keep a close eye on Nancy who was now eight months pregnant and feeling it, she looked fit to burst and was thoroughly fed up. Nancy had stopped work and was making sure everyone knew she was not a happy bunny, the house was now ready to move into, and they had Ronnie enrolled into a good secondary school everything was moving along as planned, he frowned when the only thorn in his side was Debbie, she had refused any contact with the solicitors he had even tried to contact her and got no reply, he was told the house was empty, as soon as this bit of work was over this matter was being resolved, he was getting the serious hump, Sunday could not come soon enough.

Saturday night all the men kissed their wives and children goodbye and went to their mothers for the final push, they had all the uniforms and trucks ready to go at one of the disused yards, they had to be in Hatton garden setting up at 7am none of the shops were open on Sundays so the roads in the area were deserted, the drains were already coned off and road had diversions set in place, the adrenalin was pumping through their veins, no one was going to get any sleep tonight, well apart from Stevie that fucker could sleep on a washing line, and wouldn't even wake up unless you stuck dynamite under him. Puna had made one of her legendry stews with dumplings that Adam was sure could have been used as hand grenades if the army ever got short they should reach out to his mum he remarked at the table every one cracked up, he gripped his mum and gave her a cuddle the women was a total brahma, the backbone of the family and was dearly loved by everyone. All the boys sat down at the table and the stew was served up with thick crusty slices of bread the boys got stuck in, Puna stood on the freehold of her kitchen with one of her endless cuppas in her hand and a cigarette in the other she knew what the rub was for the next few days she would not rest until her boys were all accounted for, her face showed no emotion but she was worried, this was going to be front page news Monday morning, she knew she had to put on a brave face for her boys, looking at them she knew they would be fine, the thing with having Adam at the helm was he was the brains to the point of perfection , he was extremely clever, he was analytical he could process information so quickly and have a solution for it all, that was what made him a killer in business. As the boys tucked in and mopped their bowls there was a buzz in the atmosphere, the boys were ready, they pushed their chairs back all giving each other and their dear mum a hug and made their way over to Bow.

The boys spent the night trying to get a bit of kip, playing cards and drinking copious cups of tea as the sun rose in the morning, everyone was itching to get the job underway, Adam went over everything again, the boys had formed a circle and stood shoulder to shoulder "right are we all in boys" they all nodded right let's do this!

Bobby was already on his way to the shop dress all in black full orthodox wear, muttering under his breath he always got the dodgy jobs, he walked along Hatton garden, the streets were deserted he whistled as he approached the shops and walked up the steps to the shop door, he pulled the keys out his hands already gloved up and opened the door, he let himself in and walked to the security pad and tapped in the code to reset the alarm, lovely! Bobby smiled as the alarm stopped beeping and displayed deactivated. He walked to the back office keyed in the code to the large safe and opened the door he whistled slowly the trays of jewellery were stacked high, he left it open and walked down the stairs and opened the safety deposit room the door was at least a foot deep and was heavy to pull open he pulled it slowly and walked over to the deep box 339 and marked it this was the box with the ruby and the Faberge eggs in, the boys had lock punchers made especially for the safety deposit boxes. Bobby started punching the locks moving swiftly from one box to the other he had two hours to crack as many open as he could he had a bet that he would get over four hundred he had put a monkey on it with the boys, being the fittest out of the brothers he was punching the locks through with ease, Adam and Stevie would be here in a hour to start emptying the boxes and bagging it up and by the sound of it he could hear the boys were working their way through underneath it was all working like clockwork. Bobby looked at his watched and put his clothes back on and walked to the front of the shop where he knew Adam and Pauly was waiting, he unlocked the door and let them in they were dressed in high vis and looked the part, the workman were here, "come on boys let's get cracking" Pauly went to the safe and methodically started to clear the boxes and bag the contents up and cable tie them, he worked quietly and smoothly they had practised this so much they worked synchronized as one, Adam was in the safety deposit room and clearing the boxes Bobby had punched all the boxes through and was now collecting the bags and pushing them through the smashed out toilet they were dropping down the pipe straight into a large bin, the boys had wheels attached to the bottom and as one was filling the other was being pulled to the large pipe that was pumping the bags up into the tanker above they had thirty minutes left Stevie shouted up to Adam "how's it looking" Adam looked around they were nearly done, all the practise had paid off, the safe and ninety percent of the safety deposit boxes were emptied when they had cracked open the Faberge safety deposit box Adams heart had sang the ruby alone was going to set them up, it was obviously Russian, Mary had given them the earn of a lifetime. As they finished off the last bits Bobby was getting ready to put his hat back on, he had bagged up the CCTV tapes and sent them down the chute, being the crank that he was he inserted a Disney video into the vhs player and chuckled picturing the old bills face when they played it back! Adam and Pauly finished up and left the shop first, they walked around to the truck that had just finished pumping up the last piece of jewellery how they got the gold bars up he would never know but they had, they cleared everything away and jumped in the truck, the relief they felt that the first part was completed was overwhelming.

As they drove past the shop they spotted Bobby locking up it was like they had never been there, they knew the timeframe was working in their favour by the time they discovered that the shop had been done the truck would already making its way to Spain and going to Freddie. As they drove back down the A13 and towards Dartford, the mood in the truck was unreal, but no corks were going to be popped until the truck was safely in Freddie's compound, some of the boys were already there. Adam would join them in a few days, his thoughts went to Nancy he had four weeks left and his baby would be here, everything was good, they drove past Dagenham and onto the Tilbury docks, they cleared through the port with ease and drove into a large industrial building, Danny was waiting for them and directed them to the container, they drove the truck straight in and turned the engine off, Adam cleaned the truck with the boys from one end to the other, they all had their gloves on still but he wanted to make sure there was no room for mistakes he even made them wear hair nets under their work hats he didn't want to leave a trace once he was fully satisfied he stepped back, no police, no one was hurt, and nobody one knows, could they have just pulled off the perfect job?

The boys left the container with Danny he made sure it was loaded on a ship that was going over to Spain and he joined the boat with Brian as workers mates, to keep a close eye on it, everyone went to Chelmsford, they stripped and everything was put in the Furness, they put the kettle on everyone was buzzing it had been done better than expected, "right boys stick with the plan and we will see the dividends in around 10-12 weeks, right I'm off home I have a very pregnant fiancée to butter up and make happy" the boys laughed knowing that they were all going home to a similar welcome from their missus.

Adam made his way home, he was absolutely made up he knew once that door was opened on Monday all hell was going to break loose one of the boys had been sent to Mary to tell her it was done she knew the score and was ready there was nothing that led back to her, they didn't have a clue and the icing on the cake was old Rubin had expired in his sleep so they would never know what she had access too.

He speed through to Bethnal Green, he was starving hungry and had asked Mrs Swan to make them a lovely three course meal at the house in Holland park, he pulled up and waved at Sue she waved back "you're in the dog house" he laughed and sprinted up the stairs, he burst through the door and shouted for the girls, Ronnie come steaming down the stairs and threw herself into Adams open arms "thank god mum has been a right pain in the ass" as she said it Nancy come lumbering down the stairs it was now getting uncomfortable she wanted the last four weeks to get a move on she was fit to burst and couldn't see her feet, she felt like a right lump, Adam was looking at her thinking the complete opposite she was glowing absolutely beautiful, she was the mother of his child and he loved her beyond what he thought he could ever feel, he scooped her up in his arms and kissed her deeply he could feel her melting into his arms," don't leave me no more I can't do this on my own I'm feeling really vulnerable" he nodded and kissed her again, "ok babe, let's go were off to Holland park Mrs swan has been cooking up a storm and has made you a lovely dinner, what do you say we stay there tonight?" She looked at her Adam "I would sleep anywhere with you from Holland park to under a railway bridge" he kissed her on the tip of her nose "and that's why I love you" they packed a bag and drove to Holland park and were chatting away happily in the car as they made their way through London, neither of them spotted the Mercedes following them a few cars back. It parked up and watched them go into the new house, the driver got out and stood in the park opposite, he sat there in the dark smoking watching the happy family through their living room window, they had no idea that in a few days their life was going to change for ever, the plan was already set in motion all they needed now was opportunity as there was no going back............

Monday morning, Mr Afifi was walking to work, he had a shipment of diamonds in the safe that he wanted to set in some platinum bands that he had been working on the stones were flawless and would pull in a good profit, as he walked up the stairs and opened the shop door he punched in the alarm code and reset the alarm, he was humming as he walked through to the back office, as his eyes registered the upheaval in front of him, he dropped his keys in shock and run to the desk to press alarm that was underneath, the shop was emptied his legs went weak everything was gone!

By noon it was all over the news they didn't have any estimate on how much was stolen all the staff was trying to get the records for the police, forensics were crawling over the shop with a fine tooth comb, the staff would have to be interviewed individually, Mr Afifi was in complete shock, he could not talk about the loose diamonds in the safe, they were not on the paperwork, they were not insured and not exactly kosher was putting it mildly, he knew that the chance of finding the stones or contents of the shop and safety boxes was slim to none, he knew he was finished, when he pictured the safety deposit room he can feel the bile rising in his throat he had long since lost the contents of his stomach in the bin next to his desk, even when the insurance paid out he didn't know if he would ever recover from this.

Adam and Stevie were reading the papers in the offices in silence the filth were running around like headless chickens, they had already spun a few blaggers but had drawn a blank, the boys were not even in the picture, Linda walked into the office and told Adam to call Freddie, Adams brow creased he already knew the truck was being unloaded and that the boys were taking the stock to pieces, he picked up the phone and gave Freddie a quick bell, "you ok my old mucker?" "listen you need to get on a plane and come over today, no fucking about, I need you here by tonight" "is everything alright?" Adams brow creased with concern "it will be when you get here, listen I don't want to say anymore but get her as fast as you can" Freddie put the phone down, he picked the ruby up his heart was racing, this was going to Singapore he was shaking as he examined the stone the fire and sparkle was the best he had ever seen, this stone was significant and he knew he would never hold another in his hand like this in his lifetime, he sighed the boys had hit the jackpot.

This haul was a lot more then he had anticipated the Faberge eggs were already gone they had been sent to the Emirates, he had received the money through a wire transfer, Adam was the brains and had thought of everything, that's why he had to come over and help him. Adam spoke to all the brothers and told them what was going down he didn't want to leave Nancy but had no other choice, Puna had agreed to move in with her until he got back home and the Aunties would be by her side, he knew that the family would watch over her and protect her, it was the only way, but he also knew she would probably serve him his balls on a platter for this. He left the club with Stevie who drove him back to the flat, "are you coming up" Stevie laughed "nah mate fuck that you're on your own with this one" Adam shook his head he didn't blame him on that score "cheers bruv" Adam jumped from the car and walked up the stairs. Luckily Puna was already on her way over, his heart was heavy but he knew he had to go over to Freddie. Once the graft was cleared and sent out he could sit back and spend some quality time with his little family, as he let himself in he walked into the kitchen Ronnie was making a cup of tea, "hello babe let me take that into your mum you make yourself scarce for a minute" Ronnie sensing fireworks were on the horizon dashed out the flat to Aunty Sues, she knew her mums temper and didn't want to get caught in the crossfire.

Adam took the tea into the front room, Nancy was curled up on the sofa watching the television, she looked up in surprise as Adam walked into the room she looked at his face and the smile dropped, she knew, he couldn't keep anything from her "babe I have got to go the Freddie in Spain I will be gone for three days four at the most" she could feel the tears falling down her face she wasn't even angry she put her hand up to stop him "I don't understand you made me a promise and you haven't kept it" Adam was gutted "I know babe but this is so serious, I have to go to sort this out and its only me that can do it" "Puna is coming over to stay for a few days you will not be on your own, the sisters will be in and out as well, trust me that lot will keep you occupied and the days will fly by" she smiled at him weakly she had such a terrible feeling of foreboding she just could not shake it, "listen the sooner you go the sooner you will be back "just hurry home to me" she put her arms out to him and he went to her and kissed her face "I will get back as soon as I can" he helped her up off the sofa "come on then let me help you pack"

Adam was on a plane two hours later his heart was heavy, but he took comfort in the fact that his mum and sisters were already there to keep Nancy occupied. He could not wait to see old Freddie, whatever the rub was they would get it sorted he already knew that money was being wired into their swiss bank accounts, the eggs got more than even he anticipated. It didn't take long for him to fly across, he only had his carry on case so flew through customs and jumped into the waiting car, Danny looked at him "bruv you have no idea the volume of stones and gold was beyond our estimate" Freddie is overwhelmed we need more help "that's why I'm here, let's go and have a look and see what I can do to move this quicker" Adams brain was already ticking over and right now that's what the boys needed. They pulled into Freddie's old farm, Freddie walked out to greet him, "bloody hell you look knackered" Freddie laughed, he put his arm around him, and they walked into the old farmhouse together. Adam walked down to the old basement and what sat before him left him speechless, the Furness made the room stiflingly hot, but the sheer amount of gold, gemstones and jewellery was unbelievable, Freddie gripped his shoulder "did you realise what you took" Adam shrugged in fairness his intention was the ruby and the eggs, he walked over to desk and took a box from the large walk in safe that was built into side of hillside wall, it was literally like a cave!" This is why I bought this place lad you would need a shit load of dynamite to get into it", he slid open the box and Adam picked the ruby up and could not believe the size of it, Freddie laughed, "you didn't realise did you" Adam shook his head "this stone was dug out in Mozambique and was cut and used in a Russian tsarina's necklace" Freddie showed him a picture of the necklace, "we also have the tiara that's in that picture over there" Adam was trying to absorb what he was seeing his mind calculating "so what's the rub, what can I do to help" "we need to get all that gold melted down even the bars need new minting stamps put on them, listen let's get out of this heat and go upstairs and have a cuppa" as they walked back upstairs, Freddie got a brew going "I wanted you to realise how much we are going to clear from this what figure did you have in your head?" He looked at Adam "you see the two eggs did you check the swiss account today boy?" Adam shook his head "the first payment you received was an instalment" Adam spat his tea out "£2.5 million what do you mean instalment" Freddie laughed, "the eggs sold for £7.5 million boy they were rare eggs that were lost in the Russian revolution, Adam the ruby is going to push the take to over 10 million pounds, with everything downstairs I'm thinking conservatively £15-16 million" Adams mouth went dry, Freddie smiled "this my boy is what we call a game changer, I'm proud of you all, the reason I got into bed on this job was because your family never has no outsiders and that makes no room for mistakes or treachery, we have got a few days hard graft in front of us we will start early tomorrow and work in shifts" Adam was in a state of shock, he couldn't wait for the day he handed the pay-out to everyone they had no idea!

Chapter nine

In England Nancy woke up to the smell of bacon and toast, she could her the low hum of chatter, she stroked her belly the baby had kept her awake late into the night, she could not believe how lucky she was to have Adam by her side, she stretched out and put her housecoat on, she padded down the stairs and smiled Puna was knocking up some bacon sandwiches and cups of tea, she was surprised to see some of Adams sisters were already here, they all got up and gave her a kiss on the cheek it was a bit overwhelming to be honest, she loved that she now had a protective circle around her, but being a girl that had to fight her way through life alone she found it a struggle to open up. Nancy sat down and gratefully took the tea that Puna had poured out of the pot for her, "how are you feeling sweetheart" she laughed "I'm ready to pop" the girls laughed with her as mothers themselves they understood, "I know your gutted that Adam had to fly off at short notice babe but trust me he had no choice this was a seriously urgent matter" she smiled weakly "you know what it is I'm feeling vulnerable I know I have got a massive amount of support I just can't explain it, I have this horrible feeling inside that something is going to go wrong, I think it's because I have finally got everything I could ever wish for and I'm scared" the tears started to fall down her cheeks, they all surrounded her like a group of mother hens trying to sooth her nerves,

By the second day Nancy was starting to feel seriously suffocated, there were constant visitors to the flat, it was overwhelming. In the end Nancy went through Adams drawers and found the keys to his flat in Wapping she wanted to get in the bed and be left alone, she needed a good night sleep with no interruptions or cups of tea, she popped them in a small bag and took a small roll of money to get a cab and a takeaway, she walked down the stairs slowly "I'm just popping downstairs to Sue, I will be about an hour I just want to have a catch up and she has got some bits I ordered of the oysters" Puna nodded "oh tell the shop lifter I have a list of meat I want" even with all the money that flowed through the Donnelly's fingers you could not take the east end out of them they loved a bit of knock off gear "no problem I will let her know" she kissed Puna on the cheek and left the flat. Puna watched her leave and thought I will ring Adam later this girl has got the serious blues.

As Nancy walked down the stairs she breathed a sigh of relief because all the family was in and out of the flat Glen no longer sat parked up downstairs, Nancy walked to the end of the block and onto the main road, she raised her arm and hailed a black cab, it was handy living so close to the city there was always cabs flying about. The cab pulled over "where too love?" she opened the door "can you take me to Wapping please just where Hussy the butchers is" she decided to get some shopping in, it would be nice to stop at the local shops and walk the rest of the way back, as she sat back in the taxi relief flooded through her. As the cab pulled away from the pavement, she didn't notice the Mercedes pull out behind it and start following her. The drive to Wapping took ten minutes, Nancy paid the cab and stopped in the local butchers and bakers buying a bag of groceries, she started to cut through the old red brick estates to get to the flat, she was feeling a little better just having a little quiet time made her perk up, I will ring Puna when I get back to flat and let her know I'm spending the night there, she would go nuts but she knew she would get over it. Adam was going to be home in a few days she wanted to get to Holland park and start making it her own, she had that nesting feeling now. The bag was getting heavy and she started to slow down, she was counting down now she had become so big, she thought it was a boy as she didn't remember being this big with Ronnie, as she went to step off the pavement a car pulled up and undid its window, she bent down to see who it was she got the shock of her life she stepped back in fright "Billy what the hell are you doing here" he laughed his white teeth in contrast to his deep tan, "I have a bit of business in London, and I'm waiting on seeing Adam his not back yet is he?" she shook her head, if he knew Adam was not here he must be in contact with them "jump in I will give you a lift to the flat I am going that way so it's no problem you look fit to burst, trust me, we have sorted out our differences there is no hard feelings" Billy looked so sincere she hesitated and looked down the road, the bag was digging into her palm, and her feet were rubbing against the shoes where they were starting to swell, he jumped out and opened the door, "here let me put that bag in the boot" he was smiling kindly at her, she hesitated but her feet were throbbing so bad she looked at him and smiled, he took the bag and she sat in the car with relief her feet was killing her and her belly was hanging low, she closed the door and he walked round to the car as he set off she looked out of the passenger window as the sun was glaring through the windshield, before she could turn to Billy the first punch connected with the side of her head making her smack into the car door she didn't feel the second punch she was already unconscious, her hands wrapped instinctively around her stomach he moved her head to the side so it looked like she was sleeping and whistled as he drove to Essex.

Nancy come too and gingerly touched the side of her head, she had a splitting headache and winced when she run her fingers over her temple, she had a huge bruise and open cut in her hairline, she looked around, her eyes took a moment to get accustomed to the lack of light, there was a bed, a toilet in the corner, a table, with a small television on it and that was it, it was more of a container the walls were made of metal. She heard a key being turned in the lock and looked towards the door, as it opened a women walked in the room she turned and closed the door behind her, Nancy looked at the sharply dressed women and could feel her heartbeat rising in her chest, years on the street had taught her not to show fear, her face showed no emotion, Debbie looked at Nancy coldly assessing her from head to toe, "I am Debbie Donnelly, and you are the infamous Nancy" Nancy sat back on the bed and watched her captor silently, Debbie looked around the room, "I'm going to be straight with you from the get go, when I first found out about you I just thought you were a passing fling and he would soon bore with you, then the weeks became months and he started pressing me for a divorce" she smiled showing perfect white teeth "that will never happen, but you got me curious, I wanted to know what all the urgency was about and decided to find you and get a good look at you, imagine to my surprise to see you pregnant, you see I could never have children and I knew that you being knocked up was the death bell for our marriage, and that I had lost Adam forever, believe it or not I loved Adam, but you took him from me" she placed her hand on the television "at first I was just going to wipe you out, but then I thought no that's not enough I want you both to hurt like I have, so I've decided to give you a choice you can die now or" she pointed at Nancy's stomach "you and your unborn child can stay here in this room that I had specially built for you and have the child which I will take, and you die, that is your choice today you either sacrifice your child and give it to me, or I go and get one of the shotguns and happily put a bullet through you right now and burn this place to the ground" Debbie turned on her heel pointing to the corner "there is food and water in that little fridge over there, I will come back in the morning and you can give me your decision, sweet dreams" she opened the door and walked out locking it behind her, humming to herself as she walked out of the old barn, she walked back to the house with a spring in her step.

Nancy slumped back on the bed, she was so scared she started to shake in shock, she had to slow herself down and control her breathing, placing a protective hand over her stomach, Debbie was obviously a very disturbed women, but she had the upper hand, she was locked up and pregnant, obviously she was going to agree to her that way it bought Adam some time, he would turn the streets upside down and empty their pockets to find her this she was sure of, she walked to the fridge and poured out a glass of water, her head was absolutely throbbing, she touched her hairline and could feel it was still wet with her blood, she looked around for anything that could be used as a weapon there was nothing, frustrated she laid down on the bed, and tried to remain calm, this bitch had under estimated her, she had lived a childhood locked in a room and she escaped that she could do it again, all it took was opportunity and one will come she reassured herself.

Adam was shouting down the phone at anyone that would listen "what do you mean you can't find Nancy!" He was bellowing so loud the boys stopped work and walked into the villa, Freddie put the kettle on and started the tea silently listening to Adam, "your telling me you have checked the houses flats and hospitals and you can find my Nancy, how the fuck did you lose a heavily pregnant women" the fear was trickling through his body, alarm bells were ringing "I'm coming home now I will get the next flight out" as he turned round he was surprised to see Freddy was already standing there with his bag and the car keys in his hand "come on boy let's get you home we will leave these two here, I'm coming with you" Adam nodded he was struck dumb by the latest turn of events, where the fuck was Nancy?

As the two men sped towards the airport, Nancy was sitting at the table in the room, after a restless night she was ready for the bitch to come back the fear she had felt had slowly turned to fury, she has realised it was Billy that had got her to this point so they were in this together, she would personally rip his balls off and serve them to him on a skewer. She knew by now the family would be looking for her and would leave no stone unturned, she had tried to calculate how long it would be before Adam got back home knowing Adam he was already on his way this gave her some comfort, her head still throbbed and she had been sick a couple of times, she put it down to fear, she was jolted from her thoughts from the noise of the key turning in the lock, in walked Debbie in a cloud of rive gauche, dressed in a slim red suit, she looked down at Nancy, who was looking grubby and seriously pissed off and smiled "so have we had a little think about last night" Nancy looked up at her with murder in her heart "of course I'm going to save my baby, the baby that I made with Adam a baby made out of love" she looked up at Debbie, "Adam will leave no stone unturned to find me and OUR child, how about I give you a choice you let me out of here, and I will never tell him what has happened here", she looked up at Debbie who threw her head back and laughed "you are hardly in the position to negotiate, and they will never find you here, I have brought you some breakfast now eat up, we don't want you getting sick do we" she looked at Nancy's stomach she craved that child so much it consumed her every thought.

Debbie was sure Adam would never find her, she had a house left to her many years ago from her dear aunty, she had never told Adam at the time she was left it as she had been hospitalised, she had a nursery ready and the house was completely redecorated she had everything in place just to disappear without a trace she was happy in the knowledge that they would never find her, she had enough money to see her through ten times over, she had emptied the accounts out sold all her jewellery and was sitting on a very healthy nest egg, she turned around and walked out of the room smiling as she locked the door, Nancy sat back in the chair, the tears welled up in frustration, please god Adam find me before this nut case really loses the plot.

Adam and Freddy got off the plane and walked through customs quickly they were met by Stevie and Dennis, Adam was breathing fire on the plane ride back across it had taken a lot of scotch and Freddy reassuring him that they would find her to calm him down, as he looked at his brothers face they shook their heads to the unasked question, nothing, they had been everywhere they had one sighting in Wapping but that was not confirmed, they jumped in the jag and drove silently along the motorway and then onto the A13 "tell me what you know so far" Stevie cleared his throat "little Glen has been everywhere, big Dave is with Puna and Bobby, everyone is waiting at Spring Walk, we know that she was in Wapping, she had bought some shopping at Hussy's and the local shops, but she never got to the flat" Adam could feel the blood draining from his face, "get me to Spring Walk" Stevie put his foot down on the accelerator and the jag growled and booted full throttle to East London.

Adam waked in to Puna's fit to explode, everyone was crammed into the small house, all the security, big Dave was at the front, he had ripped the West End apart for Nancy he had made it his mission to set the bongo drums in motion every snitch, informant and working girl was now aware that Nancy was missing and there was a large chunk of change waiting for information, London was buzzing with the news, everyone had their ear to the ground, Dave was sure that news would start to trickle in and he would investigate every drop with a magnifying glass until he had his boss back safe, he nodded at Adam and gripped him in a tight bear hug, Adam looked around all the anger dropped from him in an instant, this was his family, his people and they were there for him and Nancy, "where's Ronnie," Glen spoke up first "she is with her Aunt Sue she won't leave her side, Puna has been at the flat, she come back her for this meet and I will take her back, Ronnie knows something is wrong but doesn't know what, we have kept her surrounded so she is protected, Tyrone is keeping a close eye on her too" he nodded, he was at a loss everyone knew the unspoken rule women and children were off limits in their world so whoever had taken his Nancy must have had a deep vendetta with Adam or his family and the thing was he couldn't see who that was and that was what bothered him more than anything he was baffled. Dave cleared his throat and started telling him what was already being put into action, he nodded the women were going back to the flat in Tomlinson close, Mrs swan was at the house in Holland park with Jimmy, and the boys were now splitting and hitting the pavement it was time to get in the boozers, go and see anyone that had an axe to grind with the family, Dave stepped up to Adam and put his arm around his shoulder "bruv we have got this, we will leave no stone unturned, were going to the Ship and Shovel on the A13 all the Rainham and Essex boys meet up on a Friday, and they work all over the smoke, you take the jug house in Ben Johnson road, Stevie you go to the Horse and Groom near Brick Lane" they all nodded as Dave read out the list of pubs, Adam watched as everyone left for their destination like their ass's were on fire, he had to hand it to Dave he wasn't messing about he had this organised like Colonel Custer and the last stand, he didn't like the way this was making him feel he was in unchartered territory and was glad that Dave had took over, he knew he was close to losing control of his emotions and until his dying day he would be forever in this big man's debt.

Chapter ten

Nancy was not a happy bunny she ate the food and managed to have a wash down she even sat and watched the television that the nutty bitch had set up for her, she knew that by now Adam would be back on home turf and would be ripping London apart looking for her, she knew she was not in London she had heard no sirens nothing for the days she had been here, she placed her hand on her stomach the baby had dropped down, she had tried to remain calm but she was close to tears she grimaced in pain she thought she was having some Braxton hicks her belly was so tight, as she pulled a face and clutched the side of the bed, she felt like she had wet herself she looked down at the pool of water on the floor in amazement, it was too soon! she wanted to cry she was now frightened if she had this baby here that lunatic would surely kill her, her head was throbbing, she knew the shock of being abducted had finally taken a toll.

As if on cue Debbie was walking in with a tray of food and cold drink, she looked at Nancy and put the tray down and hurried over to her, she went to place her hand on Nancy's stomach Nancy pushed her away "don't touch me" she growled Debbie was taken aback at the menace in Nancy's voice she pushed her shoulders back "do you think the baby's coming" Nancy looked up at her and she knew that this was the only opportunity she was going to get, the door was left unlocked where Debbie had rushed in, Nancy doubled over in pain "my waters have broken and I am having contractions" Debbie looked over her shoulders and see the wet floor her face was flush with excitement "let me sort the bed out and we will get you comfortable" Nancy knew it was now or never and seized the moment she picked up the chair and with every ounce of strength she walloped it across Debbie's back, Debbie fell to the floor, knocked out, her slight frame had taken a serious blow, she gave her one final blow and dropped the chair. Nancy snatched the keys from the table and run from the room, as she stepped outside the metal door she looked around and realised she was in a barn, she kept running holding the bottom of her stomach, stopping and holding onto the barn door when the contraction came, taking a deep breath she pulled the door open she tried to cover her eyes and squinted as she got accustomed to the bright sunlight the pain in her head was now searing. Nancy looked around, her heart sunk as she run out she was surrounded by fields there was nothing else she run to the back of the barn and spotted a large land rover she looked down at the keys and realised that the car keys were not on them so she kept on running through the fields, barefoot and gripped with absolute terror, she held on to her low stomach as she climbed over the first fence, her feet were cut from the rough ground but she didn't care the adrenalin had made her numb she kept going heading as fast as her feet would take her to the tree line.

Debbie was disorientated, shaking her head, what just happened? then she realised where she was, that bitch! she jumped up and sprinted to the corner of the barn and grabbed a pitch fork from the barn wall, screaming "I'm going to fucking kill that bitch" she ran outside and looked across the fields and couldn't spot her, she ran to the back of the out buildings and see Nancy stumbling to the treeline, Debbie gripped the fork in both hands and gave chase.

Everyone was doing their part, the streets were buzzing with the gossip Adam Donnelly's girl had been taken, vanished off the face off the earth, there was a serious amount of wedge on offer to anyone that had any information, but for once people were scratching their heads, big Dave was in the Ship and Shovel talking to the local Essex faces, they had put the feelers about and drawn a blank, as Dave was propping up the bar Wesley walked into the bar, he was a butcher by trade and had a business in Smithfield he served a lot of bars and restaurants around Essex and the surrounding areas, as he ordered a pint and sat down his ears twitched at the conversation that was taking place next to him, he sipped his pint slowly digesting the fact that Adams girl had been lifted, Wesley spoke to a lot of punters on a daily basis, and remembered a nugget of information that he had heard from a little bistro in the back of Chelmsford, it was near great Witham if he remembered rightly he left his pint and walked over to the pay phone keeping a beady eye on big Dave as he spoke quietly on the phone, one thing about Wesley when he spoke he made sure it was from the horse's mouth, he thanked Carole who confirmed what he had remembered and placed the phone back on the hook and walked slowly over to Dave, "you got a minute fella" Wesley lifted his pint and Dave followed him to a quiet corner, "listen I'm not sure if this is related to Nancy, but I heard a nugget a few weeks back, he slid a card over with a phone number and name on it, that's Carole she is the owner of a little bistro I supply she told me she spotted that pimp Billy that Adam outed sitting in a deep conversation with an older women" as Wesley described her, Dave felt the penny drop in his head and his ass dropped out, he had spotted that ponce Billy a couple of weeks ago in a Mercedes outside the pub he wracked his brain trying to think, he tried to play it out in slow motion in his head picturing him drive past he was not 100% sure, but his instincts told him this was the break they were waiting on, he had a serious beef with Adam and Nancy he shook Wesley's hand "mate I think you have just cracked it, we will come and find you ok" "Wesley shook his head "nah don't you worry about any of that boy, you go find that girl" Dave gripped his shoulder and nodded and run to the phone that was by the side of the bar, the bongo drums were beating loud they now had a name.

Within half an hour of the phone call the Donnelly's had put fifty grand on Billy's head, any information that lead to his whereabouts, every snitch, and face were now on the blowers or pounding the pavement it had now become a mission with the men, they all had the same beliefs you don't involve the women or kids, it didn't take long for information to trickle in, they jumped in the car and were making their way to a house in south street Rainham, word had it this is where Billy was putting his head down, as they raced down the A13 Adam was praying to himself hoping that Nancy and the baby was ok, he was perspiring heavily he had never felt fear like what he was feeling right now, please god let her be ok.

As Adam raced towards Rainham, Nancy was running for her life, she had made it to the treeline, her head was pounding, her feet were cut to pieces, she had shooting pains running through her body, she knew Debbie was catching up behind her and she couldn't afford to stop so she kept pushing holding onto her stomach for dear life she could feel she had wet herself and looked down, her night dress was covered in blood her legs were slick, she was now crying freely, she knew she couldn't stop she could hear cars and ran towards the noise she was terrified, she ran up a steep bank her head was spinning and lost her footing slipping down a steep incline she tried to slide down on her bottom, her eyes wild with fear she looked up behind her and see Debbie with the pitchfork in her hand, it was the push that Nancy needed, she ran through the clearing towards the noise of the cars, still looking behind her she tripped and fell forward, as she fell to the ground she put her hands out to soften the blow, landing heavily she banged her head off the concrete curbing and sunk into the darkness that took her.

Noreen Stewart and her husband were driving back through Witham when Noreen spotted something coming out of the dense treeline, "Edward slow down" she shouted, she could not believe her eyes a heavily pregnant women covered in blood came tumbling out of the trees and fell, it was like slow motion watching her bounce down the bank and onto the tarmac, her hand flew to her mouth trying to stifle the scream of shock when the poor girls head hit the pavement, "quick pull over!" the girl didn't move Edward pulled over safely to the side of the road and so did a lorry, Noreen pulled a blanket from the boot of the car, "quickly Edward this women is unconscious" she noted the blood coming out of her mouth, she bent down to cover her up they heard a noise coming from the trees and looked up but could not see anything, the lorry driver jumped out and shouted there's a phone further down I'm going to call for help, he ran to his truck and pulled off at speed, Noreen looked at the heavily pregnant women that was covered in cuts and filthy dirty, she had a deep cut to her forehead, her legs were covered with blood, she ripped the sleeve off her blouse and pressed it to her head, she felt for a pulse and prayed to herself thanking the lord when she found a faint one, please god let this dear girls child survive this, she held onto the girl for dear life and prayed for the ambulance to come.

Debbie stood in the back of the trees watching as people got out of their cars and ran to help Nancy, she heard the ambulance siren and hid further back, as the paramedics ran towards her and started trying to revive Nancy, she strained to hear them talking "what do you think, that's a bad head injury we need to get her to the hospital now and get this baby out of her, she is bleeding heavily, I think she is slipping away" as they picked Nancy up and put her into the back of that ambulance, Debbie dropped the pitchfork to the ground and like a robot slowly started making her way back across the field it was over.

Adam was racing to Rainham with his brothers and Dave. Stevie had only just had a phone installed in the car the week before and for once in his life he was eternally grateful, as the phone rang Adam snatched up the phone, Brian spoke "come to the yard we have got him" Adam tapped Stevie and swirled him finger in the air, "don't touch him his mine, his in the yard" Stevie nodded and turned the car off and cut through Romford to Barking like the devil himself was chasing him, taking red lights and stepping on the accelerator like his life depended on it. Within minutes they were pulling into the yard, everyone was there, Adam jumped from the car and ran towards the lock up, seeing Billy sitting there bloodied but smug was his undoing, he ran at him and picked him up by the neck of his shirt "what did you do!" he was shaking "You bastard where's my Nancy" Billy knew whatever happened he was not getting out of this yard alive he looked at Adam his eyes glinting with maliciousness, "I took her, you will find her but probably in pieces" he laughed, "you think your such a fucking prince well look at you now" Adam grabbed Bills face with both of his hands and pushed his thumb into his eyeball Billy was screaming as Adam demolished his eye, "I'm going to take you apart piece by fucking piece and then I'm going to kill every living member of your fucking family, I will wipe you off the face off the earth you shower of shite" he walked to the side of the lock up and picked up a pair of bolt croppers, the men stood there as one, Adam removed Billy's fingers and toes. Billy was delirious he had fainted twice in agony as he bled out onto the dirty concrete floor, Dave was on hand with a needle, "now I can finish you off and take away the pain see that there" waving the needle under his one eye, "I'm giving you the chance to drift off on a nice cloud of smack now give me a name or a location" Billy was defeated his blood was running in rivers around him, he opened his mouth to speak and Adam leaned in knowing he was taking the dying man's last words, "Debbie has got her, please give me the needle" Adam jumped back in shock as Dave walked towards him he held his hand up, fuck the needle, he took a large hunting knife off the side and slit his throat from ear to ear, as Billy bled out for the final time, Adam took a can of petrol and splashed it over his body, stripping every item of clothing off he threw them on to what was left of Billy and lit a match, he stood there naked as he burned, no one spoke as the flames reduced his body to nothing, they realised at that moment that Adam was the true governor.

Adam walked from the lock up to the porter cabins quickly showering and throwing on a change of clothes that he always kept in every office, he picked up the phone and made a quick call, as he put the phone down he turned to his trusted friend "Dave watch that cunt burn and make sure everything is reduced to ash then get Brian to dig the whole thing out and put it on the back of the low loader, take it to our old pal Paddy his already set it to go into some foundations being laid in the docklands tonight" Dave nodded sagely, "leave everything with me boss, and then I will be coming to where ever you are ok, whatever goes down I'm by your side" Adam looked at him he was choked but he had to hold himself together, "I've got to go, will keep you posted" as he jumped in the car, they drove towards Chigwell.

Debbie was also back at the house in Chigwell, she had left a letter for Adam as she drunk neat scotch with tears running down her face she had taken all of the medication she could lay her hands on and could start to feel herself going sideways as it slowly worked its way into her system, she watched the video tape of her wedding and cried as she walked to the back of the house. She opened the doors and stumbled unsteadily to the pool slowly walking in, welcoming the cold water that engulfed her, the tears started to roll down her face as she felt herself drifting away, she laid back and closed her eyes for the final time picturing Adam in her mind as she slowly sunk to the bottom of the pool.

Adam was making his way through Pudding Lane and quickly turned into his old road, he was surprised to see the gates were open, as the boys drove down the winding drive they were shocked to see the state of the grounds, they pulled up by the stables and run through the open front door, the stench was the first thing that hit them, there was rubbish strewn everywhere. They ran and checked each room, Adam opened his old office door and his heart stopped there were large glossy pictures on the wall of him and Nancy, her face had been scratched out and Debbie had wrote WHORE in lipstick all over the walls, he walked around speechless, there was a large amount of cash on the desk and an envelope addressed to Adam on top, he opened it quietly reading as he got to the last paragraph Stevie shouted "Adam you have got to come and see this!" Adam ran down the stairs with the letter in his hand "I know where Nancy is" he stopped talking as he followed the gaze of his brother, Debbie was at the bottom of the pool in her wedding dress floating like a macabre angel her eyes open staring up, Adam looked down at her body and felt nothing as far as he was concerned that bitch had got off lightly "listen ring Dave and get him over here with a clean-up team and ring mum and the sisters she was took to Broomfield hospital, Dennis you stay here until Dave gets here and get this place cleared, you know the score" even at a time like this Adam was conscious of the repercussions so wanted this place looking like a show home, Adam and Stevie sprinted to the car, and spun the car at speed up the gravel drive and made their way to Chelmsford.

Chapter eleven

Nancy had been rushed to hospital where the paramedics fought to keep her alive in the back of the ambulance they had a police escort that was clearing the road ahead, the paramedic knew the odds were slim to none for the girl, they just prayed the child would live, she was haemorrhaging heavily, the doctors and team were waiting outside the emergency room as the ambulance stopped and they pulled the door open the paramedic screamed "this baby has got to come out of her now it's in distress and her stats are falling" they grabbed the stretcher and ran with it "does anyone know who she is" the nurse looked at the police and ambulance crew as they raced alongside her pushing her at speed to the operating room "there's no identification on her" the police officer shook his head and looked at the poor girl whose face was now swollen and unrecognisable, they stopped at the doors as they saw the doctors waiting with their gowns and faces covered, hands raised covered with gloves "right what have we got here, the paramedic stood back and read off everything as the nurses stripped her off and started disinfecting her stomach with chlorhexidine, the doctor looked at the women is she stable enough to be anesthetized? Barely we have no choice we either loose one or both so let's do this" working quickly they incubated her, they had the tubes in and the breathing apparatus took over, the doctor looked up at the monitors before making the first incision, he stopped and watched her blood pressure it didn't drop so he continued to cut through abdominal muscles and into the uterus, the doctor worked tirelessly for ten minutes before pulling out a beautiful baby boy, he had a pulse, there was a collective look of relief, at least one of them had come out of this alive, he handed the child over to the nurses and paediatrician and set about slowly stitching the patient back up, they cleared the babies air ways with some suction and he showed his clear disapproval with a lusty cry from his well-developed lungs everyone smiled "I want her brain and body scanned as soon as she is stitched up and stable enough to move" he looked down at Nancy and sighed "it's not looking good we need to know what else is going on with her" the nurse gently wrapped up the baby with his silky black raven black hair and thought what a gorgeous baby, she put him in his little crib and with another nurse beside her started to wheel him to the maternity ward, the police officers that were standing outside looked into the little bassinette and smiled down at the little fella "I will let the station know the child's ok any news on the mother?" the nurse smiled sadly "she is in a bad way, they are just doing the x-rays now, they will keep you updated" she walked off with the other nurse remarking on what a miracle the child was the mother was smashed up and had bleed badly and the child was born without a scratch.

Adam ran to reception and described Nancy to the lady that sat behind the desk, she picked up the phone and called through to the intensive care unit, listening quietly and looking up at this hulk of a man, she stood up and ushered him and Stevie into the family room not able to look him in the face she looked at Stevie and said gently "the doctor will be along shortly ok" this scared Adam more than having a gun stuck in his face, as he paced up and down, the door swung open and the doctor still with the operation garb on, come in and shut the door, "what does your partner look like" Adam described Nancy and the doctors heart sunk this was the worst part of the job, "you have to be strong your partner has extensive injuries, we have to move quickly, please come with me" turning to Stevie the doctor nodded towards the policemen "maybe you can speak to the officers as they have a lot of questions" Adam looked at his brother "get everyone here including little Ronnie" he had seen the look on the doctors face and knew that time was running out of time.

As they rushed down the corridor, Adam asked "the baby?" the doctor smiled "you have a healthy baby boy, and a good looking one at that" Adam nodded so shocked that he didn't digest the fact he was finally a father "it looks like Nancy took some serious blows to the head, she has lost a lot of blood, we are struggling to stabilise her" he stopped outside a private room, "I will be honest with you Mr?" "Donnelly" Adam replied his mouth so dry with fear he could barely get the words out, "it's not looking good, she had a stroke as we took her off the operating table we don't know how severe it is, it looks like she held on until the baby was born with every ounce of her being, but she is in the best place and we will fight for her" he placed his hand on his shoulder, "I will be right here ok" Adam turned towards the door and pushed it open walking purposely towards the bed, there was nurses and equipment everywhere, as he walked up to Nancy his legs buckled under him, she was unrecognisable, her face was swollen and bandaged, he walked to the side of the bed and picked up her hand, kissing it as tears silently rolled down his face, he touched her cheek gently "please Nancy don't leave me we haven't lived yet, I can't do this without you, your my life, my everything fight my baby fight for us, I love you, I have waited my whole life for you" he looked up at the sky "please god give my baby a chance" he sobbed silently into Nancy's hair, the nurses looked at each other sadly in the background, this man said more in two minutes then some women heard in a lifetime one of the nurses would remark to their mother later. Adam kissed her hand and wiped his face, whatever happened he was not leaving this room until she did, he heard a gentle tap on the door, Stevie slid in slowly with the doctor, looking at Nancy's face he hid his shock well, "everyone is here Adam, the doctor has already explained that this is a ICU unit and she is too sick to see anyone, but we have got to let Ronnie and Puna up or there will be uproar" the doctor nodded, he looked at the nurse who nodded "make it quick" Stevie slid back out and ran down the hall to get little Ronnie and his mother, he bent down and tried to prepare Ronnie for what was about to happen, "listen sweetie mummy does not look like mummy ok she has been in a bad accident her face is swollen and bruised it's going to look very scary but the baby is fine ok" Ronnie nodded holding onto her nanny Puna for dear life, Puna squeezed her hand as she looked down at her, "don't worry my darling I'm with you every step of the way ok" Puna hugged the dear child close to her, she tried to hold the tears that were threatening to fall at any moment, all the women were already aware that Nancy's condition was grave, Puna's sisters were silently praying to the lord almighty with the rosery beads in the hospital chapel, as they walked towards the door Puna squeezed Ronnie's hand a little tighter and smiled trying to reassure her, they pushed the door open and Puna's smile slid from her face dear god in heaven Nancy was unrecognisable, she was not breathing on her own machines were beeping everywhere, she was shocked to her core, looking at her son bent over the bed was the undoing of her, the tears were now flowing she hugged Ronnie to her, Adam looked up and put his hand up, Ronnie ran to him and they cried together "she is a fighter baby she won't leave us, we have so much planned" he held Nancy's hand, "Ronnie's here Nancy" Ronnie kissed her mums hand "please don't go mum, don't leave me all alone" she was sobbing as Adam put his arm around her, "you will never be alone we are going to get through this ok, now mummy needs to rest ok I promise you I will not leave her side until she is better, mum take her back to the flat Aunt Sue is there as well ok my darling" he wiped the tears of Ronnie's cheeks, "I will ring you as soon as I can ok" she nodded weakly, and kissed her mum gently before leaving the room.

The first week was without a doubt the hardest of Adams life they had found a bleed on Nancy's brain and had to operate, her beautiful hair was shaved off, he didn't care he washed her hands and body gently wherever there was not a needle and tube attached, talking quietly to her, the baby had gone home with Puna on the third day, everyone was remarking how much he looked like his mum, Adam had not even seen his own child they hadn't even decided on a name, big Dave had moved into the flat with Puna and Ronnie, he did not leave the babies side, he laughed as he told Nancy about how Dave had took Ronnie to school trying to keep everything as normal as possible, all the kids stared open mouthed at the biggest black man they had ever seen holding little Ronnie's tiny white hand and waving her off to class, they thought he was a giant.

Adam kept the conversation flowing, the doctors were in and out, her liver and kidneys were showing signs of serious damage they suspected the stroke and the loss of blood and the impact of her head hitting the concrete had all combined and starved her brain of oxygen. But this did not deter Adam he carried on, by the end of week two she had stabilised enough for them to take the breathing tube out and it made such a difference she looked so peaceful her face was still badly bruised but the swelling had started to go down, she now wore an oxygen mask. Ronnie had been in and kissed her mums face gently telling her how the baby was already ruling the roost, Adam and Ronnie laughed as they told her the story of the midwife knocking on the door and big Dave letting her in, Ronnie went home with a little spring in her step, Adam stayed with his Nancy, he sang to her, cried silently into his pillow at night but never showed the fear he felt in his heart, there were a few occasions that the priest was called in, but for whatever reason Nancy found the strength and held on, but by the end of week three she had now taken a turn for the worse she was starting to turn yellow, the doctor had sat Adam down and told him her liver was badly damaged and that it would only be a matter of time she was too weak to operate on slowly her organ were going to fail and they were powerless to stop it, he shook the doctors hand and returned back to the side of his Nancy's bed as he cried and kissed her hands, he was heartbroken, he decided to let Ronnie visit her mum one last time and watched her quietly as she told her little stories about the baby and cuddled her as she cried and kissed her mum goodbye Ronnie knew and ran to her nanny Puna arms, her sobs could be heard in the corridor, it drove the nurses to tears.

Adam laid in the bed alongside Nancy the nurses had long give up on telling Mr Donnelly what to do as he ignored them, they knew now they were giving the patient palliative care and that she didn't have long, but undeterred he carried on talking to her, stroking her face he was convinced that she could hear him, "I'm just going to the kitchen my darling I need a cup of tea" he kissed Nancy's forehead and walked slowly from the room going into the little kitchen that the nurses kindly let him use, as he boiled the kettle and threw a tea bag in the cup he stared into space he was beyond tired, his shoulders had drooped in defeat, he was pouring the hot water in the cup when a nurse burst into the kitchen "quickly we must hurry" Adam and the nurse ran the short distance to the room, there were nurses everywhere there was a flurry of activity, "get the doctor in here now" Adam ran to the side of the bed, Nancy was awake.

The relief flooded his body as he went to step towards the bed, a nurse put her hand on his arm, "Mr Donnelly she does not have long" she smiled sadly at him he nodded fixed a smile on his face and walked towards his love, pulling a chair up to the side of her he gently took her hand and with the other hand stroked her cheek, the nurse had moistened Nancy's mouth with a little sponge that had been dipped in water, the whites of her eyes were bright yellow, Adam kissed her hand "I love you my Nancy" she looked at him and opened her mouth her voice was slurred and barely legible "the baby?" "you have a beautiful baby boy waiting to meet you" she tried to smile, he had already got a nurse to call big Dave, he knew what he had to do, and was already in the car with Puna the baby and Ronnie he was racing to the hospital, "Nancy don't leave me we haven't even had a chance to live yet, I have so much planned for us, your my life I can't do this without you" she struggled to speak as a lone tear rolled down her face, she slowly slurred her words out "you have to stay strong keep my babies together" with every ounce of energy she had she formed her words "I love you Adam you have given me more then you will ever know" Nancy struggled to keep her eyes opened she was so tired, as she drifted off Adam held onto her hand "stay with me Nancy fight please I beg you" he cried silently looking at the broken women that laid before him, "they are bringing the baby now hold on my darling" the doctor took her pulse and looked at Adam sadly "there was not much more we can do, we can keep her out of pain" he nodded "please don't give her the morphine yet let her look at her baby" he couldn't breathe his heart was crushed in his chest, looking at his love, he knew she was fighting with every ounce of her being to see her children one last time, the doctor nodded and stood back, after what seemed a lifetime, Dave came in with Puna and Ronnie and the baby, flushed where they had run along the corridor, he looked at the bed and knew that the reaper was circling waiting to take Nancy to meet her maker, he nodded at his best friend, so choked up, they had known each other since nursery, he cried like a baby his heart was breaking for them all, he left the room standing guard outside, he didn't know what else to do but protect the family that was in that little room, the tears fell freely down his face, he wiped them with the back of his hand shaking his head at the thought of Nancy and how life could be so cruel.

"Nancy were all here my darling, were all here" it was like Nancy was waiting for them, with every ounce of energy she processed she slowly opened her eyes looking at Ronnie, and then at the beautiful baby boy that was in Adams arms, her family, the baby had the face of an angel, his little rosebud lips and startling blue eyes, she drunk them all in she cleared her throat "Adam, I want you to name him Robert after my grandad" he nodded, he placed the baby gently beside her, and leant down to kiss her lips, he knew she was going, "until we meet again my darling" she looked at him and whispered slowly "I will be waiting for you all" he pulled Ronnie close to him and they held her hands as she slowly took her last breath, she was finally at peace and out of pain, Puna stood back clutching her hands to her chest crying silent tears, it was a sin, no mother should have to bury a women of this age it went against nature, her heart was broken for the little family in front of her, she tapped on the door and Dave put his head in he looked at Puna and she nodded he knew then that Nancy had passed over and started to recite the lord's prayer.

Adam didn't remember how he got home from the hospital or the following week, he ended up at the little flat, there was a constant flow of people, but Dave his mum and sisters seemed to be a permanent fixture he was starting to accept that Nancy was gone, he finally decided to go downstairs and have a cuppa with Sue, she had proven to be a true friend the past few weeks, and he knew he could trust her especially when it came to little Ronnie, as he sat down at her old pine table, the irony was not lost on him, knowing that his Nancy had probably sat here a few times and spilt her guts, he sipped the tea slowly and smiled "I needed that" Sue smiled kindly, she was devastated for them all, "how do you think Ronnie is baring up" Sue smiled "that girl is stronger then you know, when is the funeral?" he swallowed it was still so painful to talk about it, "we will bury her in a weeks' time they have finally released her body she is at Tadmans, it will only be family and close friends, we want you there Sue" she nodded "it goes without saying we will be there, what are you going to do" he looked at her, and put the cup down," I can't go to the house in Holland park it's too painful, I'm going to sell it, or hold onto it for the kids as an investment, we are staying put here for the time being but there are some old Victorian houses around the corner that is a possibility I can't move Ronnie away she needs us all" she nodded in agreement, "were packed in like sardines upstairs" Sue laughed "has Dave gone home yet?" He laughed "what do you think" "how's the baby?" Adam shrugged, "I'm really struggling" Sue reached across the table "don't push the baby away, if Nancy was here what would you be doing right now" he knew in his heart they would all be together, but looking at the baby was more than even he could bare, the child was the image of his mother, he drained his tea, "thanks for everything you have done for us Sue it will never be forgotten"

As the day finally came to lay his dear Nancy to rest, Adam was already awake laying in bed he could hear the hushed tones of the Aunties and family downstairs, it was going to be a small funeral it was too raw for Adam, he looked at the suit hanging on the wardrobe and his eye caught the perfume bottles that were still sitting on the dressing table, he sat up and shook himself Nancy would be cursing him telling him to be strong for the kids, who would of thought it he had kids, he swung his legs over the side and put on his dressing gown, he could still smell her in this room, it was the comfort he needed, he tapped on Ronnie's door and walked slowly into her room, "hello my darling are you ok" she smiled and he sat down on the bed next to her, "I keep thinking she will shout and ask me to make her a tea" he laughed they both knew she was a bear with a sore head without her morning cuppa and fag, he pulled a blue box out of his dressing gown pocket, and handed it to her, she traced the name Rankins with her finger that was written in gold and opened the box slowly, nestled in the white silk lined box was a beautifully engraved locket, she looked up at him, "go on open it" he smiled, she gently opened the locket to find a picture of her mum smiling back at her, "she will always be with you, you are surrounded by family and we will always be here for you, I'm your dad and in there is your brother" she nodded she jumped up and threw herself into his arms he cuddled her, she looked at him "are you going to pick my brother up now?" He nodded slowly she understood the pain even at her young age he could see it in her eyes, "come on then let's go get your brother"

Adam walked across the hallway and opened the door that Puna now stayed in with the baby, he walked over to the crib that was by the side of the bed and finally picked up his son for the first time and cradled him in his arms, he looked at the child that looked so much like his mother, he had silky raven hair and the same bright blue eyes, even at the darkest moment he finally felt a wave of overwhelming love for the little bundle that was yawning happily in his arms, he bent down and inhaled his sweet scent, his heart belonged to these children, Ronnie stroked his soft hair and kissed his forehead, she looked up at Adam, "come on dad let's take Robert down to breakfast" he held the baby in the crook of his arm and slowly walked down the stairs and into the kitchen, Dave looked up and smiled, inside he was punching the air, finally my brother has turned a corner, Puna turned and looked at her boy and grandchildren and felt the weight lift from her heart, she walked towards him open armed and embraced them he smiled at everyone in the room, "were going to be ok, now put the kettle on let's have a cup of tea"

Country Lines

Ronnie looked in the mirror and wondered where the past twenty five years had gone, she lit a cigarette and blew the smoke at her reflection, she was now a mother of four children, how her life had changed when her mother was taken from her, trying to shake the feeling of desolation, she focused on the problems that was threatening to ruin them all.

The days of old school faces were over, retired and living off their spoils her family had finally gone legitimate. The streets had a new breed, boys with errant fathers, sick of living in poverty, hungry for money and respect, they dealt in death, crack and heroin was gripping the streets, rules and loyalty were off the table.

Ronnie's boys had been pulled into the life, trained and turned out onto the streets by their own father, it was now kill or be killed, country lines had taken her boys, she knew they were all living on borrowed time, she needed an out, one where they could all walk away clean, with no one to trust the odds were stacked against her. The river of money that her sons had generated made a lot of men rich and that greed had made her a target.

She was not going to give up, she knew she would fight to survive, and the winner would take it all, in the avenue and alleyways.

Printed in Great Britain
by Amazon

22394785R00056